Play Dead

Fargo lay on his side, trying not to breathe. He heard the footsteps approaching, timidly at first, then with growing bravado as the man thought his ambush to be successful. Only when he stood a few feet away did Fargo stir.

"Son of a . . . he's still alive!"

As the man uttered those words, Fargo moved. He kicked out, catching the man's knee. A sickening crunch echoed through the still night, followed by the man's scream of profanity as the pain shot through him, and he fell to the ground, dropping his pistol.

Fargo jumped to his feet, towering over the cringing man, who glanced at his pistol nearby.

"Don't try lifting that hogleg," Fargo said coldly. "You missed the first time. Now it's my turn . . ."

Fargo clicked the hammer, aiming right between the man's eyes.

". . . and I never miss."

THE

TRAILSMAN

#231

SALT LAKE SIREN

by

Jon Sharpe

A SIGNET BOOK

SIGNET
Published by New American Library, a division of
Penguin Putnam Inc., 375 Hudson Street,
New York, New York 10014, U.S.A.
Penguin Books Ltd, 27 Wrights Lane,
London W8 5TZ, England
Penguin Books Australia Ltd, Ringwood,
Victoria, Australia
Penguin Books Canada Ltd, 10 Alcorn Avenue,
Toronto, Ontario, Canada M4V 3B2
Penguin Books (N.Z.) Ltd, 182–190 Wairau Road,
Auckland 10, New Zealand

Penguin Books Ltd, Registered Offices:
Harmondsworth, Middlesex, England

First published by Signet, an imprint of New American Library,
a division of Penguin Putnam Inc.

First Printing, January 2001
10 9 8 7 6 5 4 3 2 1

The first chapter of this book originally appeared in *Flatwater Firebrand,*
the two hundred thirtieth volume in this series.

 REGISTERED TRADEMARK—MARCA REGISTRADA

Printed in the United States of America

PUBLISHER'S NOTE
This is a work of fiction. Names, characters, places, and incidents
either are the product of the author's imagination or are used fictitiously,
and any resemblance to actual persons, living or dead, events, or
locales is entirely coincidental.

BOOKS ARE AVAILABLE AT QUANTITY DISCOUNTS WHEN USED TO PRO-
MOTE PRODUCTS OR SERVICES. FOR INFORMATION PLEASE WRITE TO
PREMIUM MARKETING DIVISION, PENGUIN PUTNAM INC., 375 HUDSON
STREET, NEW YORK, NEW YORK 10014.

The Trailsman

Beginnings . . . they bend the tree and they mark the man. Skye Fargo was born when he was eighteen. Terror was his midwife, vengeance his first cry. Killing spawned Skye Fargo, ruthless, cold-blooded murder. Out of the acrid smoke of gunpowder still hanging in the air, he rose, cried out a promise never forgotten.

The Trailsman they began to call him all across the West: searcher, scout, hunter, the man who could see where others only looked, his skills for hire but not his soul, the man who lived each day to the fullest, yet trailed each tomorrow. Skye Fargo, the Trailsman, the seeker who could take the wildness of a land and the wanting of a woman and make them his own.

Utah Territory, 1858 —
where greed is punished . . . harshly

1

"She's the purtiest thing you ever seen, Fargo. I do declare. I'd go so far as to swear it, but I don't cotton to such things. No, sir. But let me tell you, there's nuthin' I wouldn't do for her." Moroni Clawson hiked his feet up on a rock near the campfire, then leaned back to stare up into the clear, cold Wyoming night sky. The lanky man folded his hands behind his shaggy head and let out a gusty sigh. Skye Fargo waited for 'Rone to finish reminiscing about his fiancée back in Great Salt Lake City.

In a way, Fargo did not mind. If 'Rone kept talking, it saved Fargo from having to think up fancy new compliments telling how pleased he was that the army scout had finally found the woman of his dreams. Fargo preferred to stare at the same stars 'Rone looked up at, though he doubted he saw the same things. They had been on the scout for almost a month now. Captain Simpson at Camp Floyd had hired them to map out the trail already being called the Overland by many of the pilgrims flocking from back East and heading to Oregon. The army wanted the road both mapped and safe, to keep from spending all their time rescuing stranded greenhorns.

The land was beautiful, and that bothered Fargo. Not that it was the kind of land he appreciated most, but that too many people moving through would ruin it. The night was serene. A lovesick wolf howled in the distance. Now and then the flutter of a bat sounded and its dark shape would block out some of the gorgeous smear of diamond-white stars arching across the inky sky. The spring weather was about perfect, a tad nippy but without a hint of storm in it. Just the way Fargo liked it.

And he was working to destroy it all by helping Simpson map the route to be taken by the sodbusters.

He heaved a deep sigh and closed his lake-blue eyes. Too many people spoiled everything. They dug up grassland meant for deer—and they shot so many of the grazing deer that the creatures vanished, either overhunted or having migrated to safer terrain.

"Been puttin' away everything the army's payin' me for my new wife," 'Rone rattled on.

"What are you going to do with twenty whole dollars?" Fargo asked. Simpson had not been able to pay much. Fargo and 'Rone had collected their full month's pay in advance since the captain wanted them out of camp. The rest of his soldiers had not been paid in over three months, although promise from the paymaster that scrip would be forthcoming always seemed to be for the following month.

"Twenty?" scoffed 'Rone. "Money like that's not enough for a fine woman like my Lydia. I got real money."

"Sure you do," Fargo said, smiling. He and 'Rone had partnered on and off for almost a year, and he had never seen the man with more than two nickels to rub together. True, 'Rone Clawson had vanished for a couple weeks before they met up again at Camp Floyd to take this mapping chore, but he had neither had the time to go far enough, nor had he seemed any more prosperous after he got back. 'Rone refused to discuss what he had been doing, and Fargo suspected 'Rone might have another woman in the hills somewhere nearby. Maybe a Crow squaw he didn't want to talk about.

That might be why 'Rone spoke endlessly of his Lydia Pressman back in Great Salt Lake City.

'Rone pulled out his watch and held it up so he could see the firelight reflect off its battered gold case. For a moment, Fargo thought the man was going to open it to check the time. He had never figured out why 'Rone carried the watch or why he worried so much about what time it was in the middle of the night.

Fargo glanced at the stars and quickly estimated it was just past midnight. Although he could not figure out where so many of the constellations had gotten their names, and his imagination failed when it came to finding the outlines of strange animals and ancient people, Fargo knew the stars

2

well. To the north around the two dippers ran the trail of stars he called the snake. Draco was its real name. And to the western horizon shone the smoky patch of stars called the Pleiades, near the bull constellation. The horns were easiest for Fargo to find.

But he didn't need a watch to know it was still a while until sunrise. Fargo saw 'Rone finger his watch, kiss it, and then tuck it back into his vest pocket.

"Got a picture of Lydia in the watch case?" Fargo asked.

'Rone jumped as if he had been stuck with a pin.

"No, nothin' like that," he said, sounding as guilty as a little boy with his hand stuck in the cookie jar. He put his bony hand over his watch pocket.

Fargo shrugged off the man's reaction. It didn't pay for partners to ask each other too many questions out on the trail. Besides, they were about done mapping the section of land Captain Simpson had wanted scouted, and it was time to move on. As much as Fargo liked 'Rone Clawson, it was time to head for the high country and enjoy all the joys summer brought. Alone. He wasn't up for the company of one man, let alone the hundreds to be found at either Great Salt Lake City or Camp Floyd.

"Fargo, I been meanin' to ask somethin' of you. A favor. You don't have to agree, 'less you want."

Fargo moved to the campfire and poured himself some of the boiled coffee. Whenever a man started out the way 'Rone just had, it meant trouble, and he needed fortifying from the strong brew. He took a sip, made a face, then nodded for 'Rone to continue.

'Rone dropped his feet from the rock and moved closer.

"You and me, Fargo, we hit it off good. Not just this scout but earlier, too. You're 'bout the best friend I got."

Fargo wondered if this was the right time to tell 'Rone he was parting company with him. He decided to wait a spell and see what the man was working himself up over.

"It's been good," Fargo said noncommittally.

'Rone sucked in a deep breath, then let it out in a rush, mingling it with his request.

"I want you to stand up with me when I marry Lydia. Fargo, I want you to be my best man."

"An honor," Fargo said, surprised. "Not one I thought

3

you'd offer. You don't have anyone in Great Salt Lake City?"

"My brother Abraham died of cholera three years ago. John got lost. Reckon he's dead, somewhere up here in the mountains, since no one's seen hide nor hair of him in almost eight months. But that don't matter. I'm askin' you. What do you say, Fargo?"

"What can I say?" Fargo answered, knowing the anticipated solitude of the high mountains and camaraderie with wolves and coyotes would have to wait.

Astride his Ovaro, Skye Fargo felt as if he owned the world. From the way 'Rone looked around nervously, it was clear that the feeling was his alone.

"What's wrong?" Fargo asked. "You're jumpier than a long-tailed cat lying next to a rocking chair."

"Nuthin', it's nuthin'," 'Rone said. He glanced up into the hills above Camp Floyd and then forced his attention back to the broad dirt track leading to the army fort. Unlike others, Captain Simpson had not erected wood palisades around either his main building or the score of pitched tents. He relied on constant patrols to keep the Indians out and a knee-high fence to keep the chickens inside their compound.

A sentry waved to Fargo as he rode up.

"You finished lollygagging for a month and come back to lord it over us poor foot soldiers?" the sentry asked. The broad grin on his face showed he was glad to see Fargo and Clawson return. Anything that broke the monotony of pacing back and forth counted toward making this a good day. Or at least a better one.

"If you had any money, I'd swindle it away from you after a couple of hands of five card," 'Rone chimed in. "Bet you ain't been paid since we left."

"Good thing I'm not a bettin' man," the blue-clad private said, resting his musket on the ground and leaning on it. "I hope you got the trail mapped out real good so the paymaster can get a wagon in with all our money. They wait another month to pay us and we'll *own* the United States government, lock, stock, and barrel."

Fargo had to laugh. Simpson may not have a good supply

4

line, but he kept discipline and maintained a morale among his men that had to be the envy of any commander.

"We got the maps for the captain. Permission to ride on over and give them to him?"

The private snapped to attention and gave Fargo a mock salute.

"Anything that'll get us paid or laid, I'm for it!"

Fargo and Clawson rode in to the single wood cabin in the center of Camp Floyd and dismounted. Fargo stretched his tired muscles. They had ridden long and hard the past couple of days in order to get the maps to Simpson. 'Rone wanted to strike out for Great Salt Lake City right away to marry his sweetheart. Somehow, some of the man's enthusiasm had caught Fargo's imagination, and he no longer dreaded facing so many people in the city nestled beside the Great Salt Lake.

He might not have dreaded it, but he certainly wanted it over quick enough.

" 'Rone," he said as they went to the captain's door.

"What?"

"I don't have to dress up, do I? When I'm standing up with you?"

"Shucks, Fargo, those buckskins you're wearin' will be just fine. You might want to think on a bath, though. You're mighty rank after bein' on the trail so long, and I wouldn't want any of the other guests mistakin' you for a grizzly bear."

They laughed as they went into Captain Simpson's office. The young officer looked up, his eyes ringed with dark circles from the long hours. He was thinner than Fargo remembered, as if he had lost ten or fifteen pounds just from worry.

"Captain," Fargo greeted. "We got your maps done."

'Rone fished them out and laid them on the table. "You want to look 'em over? I think we done a good job. Leastwise, Fargo did. He drew 'em up real purty. I did all the dangerous scoutin'."

Clawson's joke fell on deaf ears. Simpson pushed himself back from the desk and rubbed his eyes, then turned his attention to the two men.

"Glad to see you're prompt," Simpson said. The sandy-haired officer unfolded the maps, then compared them with the others done years earlier. For the next ten minutes, the three went over the places where the maps varied. The original ones had been drawn by John Frémont and lacked considerable detail. In places, Frémont had gotten the lay of the land flat-out wrong. This was the kind of information Simpson needed to shepherd the ever-increasing flood of wagon trains along the Overland Trail safely and successfully.

"That about does it, Captain," Fargo said when they had finished.

Simpson started to speak, then clamped his mouth shut. He sat down heavily and looked up at them. Fargo waited for the shoe to drop. The captain ought to be glad they had done their work and that he could send them on their way. Two fewer civilian scouts to pay had to help matters at a payroll-less Camp Floyd.

Fargo considered himself lucky Simpson had the money to pay them at all.

"What more you thinkin' or askin' of us, Captain?" asked 'Rone suspiciously. "Not more mappin'?"

"Not that. We're having problems with road agents. I can't find them in these mountains. Like smoke. They just drift away every time a patrol gets close to them."

"What happened?"

"The best I can determine, a wagon was robbed about six weeks back. We just found the burned frame. Two men and a woman were killed. Shot."

"Could be Crow," ventured 'Rone.

"Not likely from the way the three were murdered. Indians would have taken what they needed and left without a trace. We found whiskey bottles and wasted ammunition scattered across the crime scene."

"You have other robberies?"

"A bad one earlier on. Lost a gold shipment, which is why I think they were road agents, stealing on their way through to other parts. My men have been watching the few bands of Crow hunters, and they've stayed well away from the trail and the settlers traveling through these parts."

"Then there's no problem," Fargo said pragmatically. "If the owlhoots have left the territory, they're out of your hair."

"I hate seeing unsolved cases. And I surely don't like the idea that I've exported problems I ought to have solved so that some other commander has to deal with them."

"If you don't mind my saying so, Captain, you worry too much," 'Rone started.

The young captain smiled crookedly. "You're not the first to make that observation. It galls me not to know what happened. I'd certainly appreciate it if you could track them down."

"A six-week-old trail?" 'Rone shook his head. "That's impossible, even for Fargo."

Fargo was not known as the Trailsman for nothing. He could follow a drop of rain through a raging storm. He could find spoor overlooked by the best Indian trackers. But this time he had to agree with Clawson.

"I'm good, Captain," Fargo said, "but I'm not that good. Nobody is. Be content these highwaymen are gone and let it lie."

For a moment, Simpson said nothing. Fargo read more to the story in the man's expression. The captain finally went on.

"I got two other bodies I can't explain. They were pretty well eaten by coyotes, so I can't tell how long they'd been dead. I'm thinking they might be linked to the others."

"Where did you find them?" 'Rone looked mighty apprehensive to Fargo, but Simpson didn't catch the anxious tone.

"Up in the hills above the camp. They could have been the road agents who killed the settlers. And if they were the robbers, who killed them? Maybe they're just another pair of names on a list of victims. Problem is, they look to have been dead for quite some time."

"Might be a band of outlaws had a falling out. Been known to happen," Fargo said, watching 'Rone more than the captain. 'Rone chewed at his lower lip and shifted his weight from foot to foot, as if he wanted to turn tail and run.

"Might be," Simpson said. "Not knowing is eating me up. I might still have an unknown number of road agents hiding in the hills."

"Let 'em show their faces, Captain," suggested 'Rone. "Don't go lookin' for trouble."

7

"I want to prevent it. That's my sworn duty."

"Well, Captain, as much as we'd like to help out by stayin' around, the truth is we can't. I've got a mighty important appointment to keep over in Great Salt Lake City."

"Oh?"

"He's getting married," Fargo said.

"To the purtiest gal this side of the Mississippi River. And maybe in all of the country," 'Rone said proudly. "Fargo's gonna be my best man."

Captain Simpson heaved a sigh, then rose and brusquely shook 'Rone's hand. "Congratulations. I wish you the best of luck. If you get tired of the big city, come on back. I'll always have a place for a good scout. That goes double for you, Fargo."

Skye Fargo shook the captain's hand knowing he wasn't likely to return. He was a good scout, but after he saw 'Rone Clawson married and settled down, there were other places to explore.

On his own.

2

Fargo looked around, marvelling at the elaborate buildings in Great Salt Lake City. The Mormons had built an oasis in the middle of the desert, and while it was quite impressive it was still far from home for Fargo. There were no saloons, no gambling parlors, definitely no cribs filled with loose women anywhere to be seen. 'Rone assured him such things were around, but a footloose traveler had to look for them. Fargo held back asking further about such things since the citizens in the street eyed him strangely as it was.

Relations between the Mormons and the rest of the United States had never been good. He wondered if 'Rone would follow the Mormon tradition of having more than one wife—and what Lydia Pressman would say about sharing him with other wives. Somehow, from all 'Rone had said about the woman, Fargo did not think Lydia had anything to worry over on this account. 'Rone was in love with her and no one else.

Fargo had to chuckle. Considering 'Rone Clawson had about as much money riding in his shirt pocket as Fargo, getting married would take a considerable chunk out of the twenty silver-dollar cartwheels they had each received from Captain Simpson for their month of mapping work.

The coins jingled and reminded Fargo how thirsty he was. Ignoring the chance of finding a dance hall or a saloon selling hard liquor, he wondered where—and what—Mormons usually drank. Water got mighty boring after a while, and he knew from his time on the trail with 'Rone that they looked askance at drinking coffee.

Fargo leaned back against the white frame house, wondering if he ought to go explore the city some more. 'Rone and his fiancée might still have a powerful lot of homecoming to get through.

"Fargo!" 'Rone came out on the front porch and waved. "Get on up here and meet my Lydia. Don't be shy, now, even if she's 'bout the—"

"Purtiest thing you ever did see," Fargo finished for him.

"Does he really say that?"

Fargo stopped on the top step. He stared at Lydia Pressman.

"Excuse me for staring like that, ma'am," he said to her, tipping his hat in the woman's direction, "but I thought 'Rone was exaggerating. If anything, he didn't tell the half of it."

"Now aren't you the silver-tongued fox," Lydia said, smiling prettily. She was everything 'Rone Clawson had said and more. Fargo forced himself to stop gaping at her soft brown hair, floating like a halo around her pale oval face, where twinkling brown eyes stared openly and honestly at him. As she turned amid the soft swishing of her long skirts, he saw her figure was even more than 'Rone had hinted. Her breasts were full, her waist trim and her rump without a doubt one of the "purtiest" things he had ever seen.

Fargo grunted when 'Rone elbowed him in the chest.

"Stop gawking. You ain't been on the trail *that* long, Partner." 'Rone Clawson bore down on the "partner" to let Fargo know there were some things not to be shared, even among good friends.

"This might be the first time you didn't embroider a tale to make it sound better."

'Rone glared at him, then quickly followed Lydia into the house.

"Please, Mr. Fargo, sit over here," the lovely woman said, indicating a chair next to the love seat where she and 'Rone crowded, legs and hips pressing together intimately.

"Could I trouble you for something to drink? I'm mighty parched from the trip in and, well, that big lake out there doesn't afford a thirsty man much in the way of a drink."

"The Great Salt Lake?" Lydia chuckled. "I suspect you want more than a dipper of water. I'm sorry, but all I can offer is some tea."

"Tea?" Fargo frowned. He thought Mormons avoided anything that might be considered a stimulant.

"Brigham tea," she said, smiling prettily.

"Boiled weeds," 'Rone said more glumly. "Beats drinking nuthin' but water."

"That would be fine, Miss Pressman," Fargo said.

"Please, call me Lydia. 'Rone says you have agreed to be his best man. We should be friends." Lydia's hand brushed Fargo's, lingered for a moment, then drifted away as soft as a floating feather. She licked her lips as she stared at him in a way that was a tad more than friendly. Lydia turned from Fargo toward 'Rone, but somehow Fargo felt he remained the center of attention, and it felt mighty fine being noticed by such a lovely woman.

"But not too good," 'Rone said under his breath so low only Fargo heard, obviously worried about Fargo swooping down on his lovely fiancée like some desert predator.

Lydia rose and went out to fetch the tea from the kitchen, visible through an arched doorway. Fargo looked around and appreciated how elegant the house was. All of Great Salt Lake City seemed prosperous, but this house was especially nice. The furniture was sturdy and in good condition, tables were set with lace doilies kept in place by small, fragile, painted porcelain figurines while framed paintings kept the walls from seeming too dreary.

"You're marrying into a rich family," Fargo observed. "You up for it, 'Rone?"

"Not so rich. Lydia's parents left all this to her. They died a few months ago during the cholera epidemic that swept through Great Salt Lake City."

"Heard something about that," Fargo said. He considered the bad water and disease that went with it another reason to avoid the big cities, even ones as well kept as this one.

"Here, Mr. Fargo. Tea and some cookies I baked this morning." She held out a plate for him. Again her hand brushed his and sent a tiny thrill of intimacy surging through him. Fargo took a deep breath. He told himself Lydia was only being friendly, and he was only imagining how attracted she seemed to him. These were little things, the touches, the looks and smiles, and the twinkle in her eyes when she boldly looked at him.

"Call me Skye," he said. If he was allowed to call her by her first name in private, she ought to be permitted the same familiarity.

"What an interesting name," Lydia said. "Skye, because your eyes are as blue as the sky above?" She smiled winningly. Then the tip of her tongue moved along her lower lip slowly, as if she were tasting something more than her own flesh. She winked at him right before her tongue vanished, and then gracefully turned to 'Rone and offered him some cookies.

"An old family name," he said, gulping down the tea from the delicate bone-china cup. 'Rone had been right. Nothing but boiled weeds. It made him long for a shot of whiskey or even a battered tin cup of strong black coffee boiled until it poured like syrup.

The rest of the afternoon passed pleasantly enough. Fargo could not help noting how gracious Lydia was. He had to wonder if it was his imagination or if she really did favor him more than the man she was about to marry. Fargo pushed the notion from his head. The two of them looked right together, in spite of 'Rone's rough-hewn ways and Lydia's more civilized ones.

"We got to hurry along," 'Rone said suddenly. He touched the vest pocket where his watch rested, although he did not pull it out to check the time. Lydia put her hand over his and pressed lightly. The two exchanged grins that excluded Fargo entirely. He felt uneasy for the first time all day, as if he had intruded on a private moment.

"Where do you have to go?" Fargo asked.

"To get the marriage license and do some arrangin'," 'Rone said. He stood and held Lydia's hands in his, then almost timidly kissed her. Fargo turned away, since this was none of his business.

He went outside and waited a few minutes on the porch until 'Rone joined him, a broad grin showing off his uneven teeth.

"She's really somethin', ain't she, Fargo?"

"Everything you said and more," Fargo agreed. "Who do we have to see about a license?" He was more used to common-law marriages, since a couple might have to wait a year or more to see a preacher making a circuit around a wide-open territory. The notion of getting a piece of paper

12

declaring a man and a woman married was something of a novelty for him.

They rode through the crowded city streets to an imposing courthouse. As Fargo swung his leg over his Ovaro to dismount, he heard a mocking voice from the broad, stone courthouse steps.

"Thought a yellow belly like you'd never show his ugly face here again."

Fargo stepped around his horse and saw 'Rone Clawson face-to-face with a short, bandy-legged man dressed in fancy duds. 'Rone bumped into the man's chest, knocking him back a pace.

"I thought the town rat killer did a better job," 'Rone said, glaring at the man. "But I reckon you mighta bought him off. Isn't that what you do best, Schatten? Buy influence?"

"You're jealous because you lost the election."

Fargo stepped up, not understanding the bad blood between the men.

"Need any help, 'Rone?" he asked.

"With garbage like Lester Schatten? I should say not. He's the crookedest politician in all of Great Salt Lake City. Never was a dollar he didn't try to extort or outright steal. He'd steal pennies off a dead man's eyes."

"You can't prove any of that!" raged the short man. Schatten took two quick steps back so he could mount the courthouse steps and look 'Rone squarely in the eye. "You were always trouble, Clawson, spreading your foul lies."

"Anytime I mention your name, it's got to be foul," 'Rone said, pushing past the man. "Come on, Fargo. We got business to do." When Schatten didn't budge, 'Rone sneered at him. "Might be I have to wipe some filth off my shoes fore we do our business, but that's up to this pile of dog—"

Schatten swung at him. 'Rone ducked easily and landed three quick, short jabs into the politician's belly, doubling him over. As Schatten slid to the steps, 'Rone unleased an uppercut that straightened the man back up. When Schatten hit the ground, he was unconscious.

"Son of a bitch is crookeder 'n a dog's hind leg." 'Rone stepped over him and went into the courthouse. By the time they had the marriage license and returned, Schatten was gone.

"If he's got any kind of political power, you've got one whale of an enemy," Fargo pointed out.

"He's 'bout the most cowardly snake that ever slithered."

"Don't go stepping on rattlers unless you want to get bit," Fargo warned.

'Rone laughed lightly. "I got more important things on my mind. Like Lydia—"

'Rone Clawson stiffened as a rifle's charge rang through the air. He turned and reached out in the direction of the courthouse before he toppled over like a felled tree. For a moment, Fargo could not believe what had happened. Then he saw the red spot blossoming squarely in the middle of his friend's back. 'Rone had been shot on the Great Salt Lake City courthouse steps.

" 'Rone!" Fargo cried, dropping beside his friend.

"Partner," grated out 'Rone. "They got me. They been huntin' me and they g-got me."

"Who? Schatten?"

"See to Lydia for me. See that she doesn't want for nuthin', Fargo." 'Rone trembled like he had a high fever and then died in Fargo's arms. The Trailsman lowered his friend gently to the marble steps, then looked up for the backshooter who had foully murdered 'Rone Clawson.

Fargo swung about, his hand going for his Colt. He saw three men, one with a rifle in his hands, clustered together in the direction 'Rone had pointed before falling. When they realized he had spotted them, they bolted and ran. Fargo took off after them.

"Stop!" he shouted, but this only lit a fire under them. Two jumped on horses and rode off separately to make it harder to catch them. The third one, wearing a red plaid shirt and still on foot, slipped out his six-shooter and got off a couple of shots at Fargo, forcing him to duck back, using the building for cover. When he chanced a quick look around the corner, the man had vanished like a puff of smoke in a high wind.

Fargo started to poke around for a trail to follow, but the law had finally twigged to a crime committed on their doorstep. A half dozen Great Salt Lake City lawmen circled 'Rone's body, pointing and arguing about what to do.

14

It was as if they had never seen a dead man before, much less one murdered under their noses. Fargo took a deep breath to settle himself for the ordeal, then went to talk to the law.

The marshal looked up from 'Rone's body, eyeing Fargo from head to toe. "You know this gent?"

"He was my partner," Fargo said. "Are you the town marshal?"

"I am. My name's Gutherie. You and him have an argument?"

"He was gunned down from back there," Fargo said, pointing in the direction of the courthouse. Marshal Gutherie and his deputies all looked in that direction, but what Fargo saw the other way turned him cold with rage.

Not only had his partner been foully murdered, the killer, who had been on foot, had returned to steal 'Rone's horse.

"Horse thief!" Fargo cried. Fargo tried to push past the marshal, only to find himself held by two deputies.

"Hold on, there," Marshal Gutherie said sternly. "I'm not done talkin' to you. I got to find out what's happened here."

" 'Rone's killer's stealing his horse!" Fargo struggled and then subsided. Answering the lawman's questions was the best way to settle the matter. "Did you see him? Who was he?"

"Settle down," Marshal Gutherie said, finally looking down the street, then back at Fargo with suspicious eyes. The thief—one of 'Rone's killers—had vanished. The marshal had never even seen him. "We need to get everything squared away, then we can go chasing after runaway horses."

Fargo held his anger in check as he answered the marshal's questions. Gutherie even noted his sketchy description of the horse thief, for all the good that did, since he did not dispatch any of his deputies to chase after the man. Fargo saw Marshal Gutherie was more inclined to fill out reports than to catch criminals. After what seemed an eternity, Gutherie was satisfied that he had not shot his partner and let Fargo mount his Ovaro to ride off.

Fargo faced a real ordeal now. He had to tell Lydia Pressman her fiancé had been murdered.

3

Fargo never figured he would mount the thirteen steps to a gallows to be hanged, but he knew then how it must feel as he stood at the foot of the three steps leading to Lydia Pressman's neat, whitewashed house. He wiped his lips, then screwed up his courage and mounted those steps to the front porch.

Lydia must have heard the boards creaking, because she opened the door before he could knock. Her lovely face was aglow. Then the light faded when she saw his expression.

"Skye, what's wrong?" She looked past him. "Where's 'Rone?"

"I've got some bad news," Fargo said. He was not much good at figuring flowery ways of delivering bad news. He preferred to hear it straight out and believed Lydia would want it that way, also. "It's 'Rone. We just came out of the courthouse when he was gunned down."

"Where is he? How—" The woman's face went pale when she read the answer in Fargo's. "Dead?"

"I'm afraid so. Three owlhoots backshot him, then high-tailed it before I could catch up with them." Fargo pictured the situation perfectly in his head. The two who had ridden away were beyond his reach, but the one who had stayed on the ground had to leave a trail that could be followed by the Trailsman.

"The marshal, what's he doing?"

"Marshal Gutherie doesn't seem to know exactly what to do. I get the idea there's not much crime like this in Great Salt Lake City."

Lydia shook her head. Tears leaked from the corners of her eyes and down her cheeks, leaving salty tracks. She hastily wiped the tears off and turned away from Fargo so she could hide her grief.

"Come in, Skye, please."

"For a little while," he said. "Do you have any family or friends who can come over?"

"No family. 'Rone was all I had. But friends. Yes, friends." The way the distraught woman spoke told Fargo that Lydia had no idea where to turn for help. Then she swung about and flung her arms around him, holding him close as shudders racked her trim body. He held her awkwardly, not sure how best to comfort her.

"Find them, Skye, find them and don't let them get away with killing him."

"Before we went into the courthouse to get this"—he pulled the marriage license from his pocket and gave it to her—"'Rone got into an argument with a man named Schatten."

"Him!" Lydia snarled the word. "He'd kill 'Rone in a flash. There's been a feud between them for years."

"I didn't see him with the men who shot 'Rone," Fargo said.

"That doesn't mean he didn't hire them. 'Rone hadn't been back in town long enough for word to get out. Besides, he didn't have that many enemies, at least not ones willing to kill him." Lydia turned her brown eyes up and stared into Fargo's azure ones. "They shot him in the back?"

Fargo nodded, not trusting himself to speak.

"Marshal Gutherie isn't the man to find them and bring them to justice. And Schatten owns him. The marshal would never cross a politician of Schatten's power."

"There's the federal marshal," Fargo began. Then he saw something harden in the woman.

"Please, Skye. You were 'Rone's best friend. Don't let his murder go unavenged. Find them—and make sure they incriminate Schatten. I *know* he's behind this. It's the kind of thing he would do!"

"The trail is getting cold," Fargo said. Lydia pushed farther away from him, clutching the now-useless marriage license in her hand.

" 'Rone said you were the best tracker in the West. If

you got to the chore right away, you'd have a better chance, wouldn't you?"

"I would," Fargo said, "but this is a matter for the law."

"Unless I miss my guess, Gutherie's already back in his office filing papers. That's what he does best."

"He said he'd arrange for the funeral with some undertaker named Carstairs. Is that all right?" Fargo felt himself being drawn in more and more to the spinning tornado surrounding 'Rone Clawson's murder, and he was not sure it was his place. 'Rone had been his partner, but Fargo had no idea what the man had been involved in or if it was even his place to go digging into the man's affairs to find out.

Lydia nodded, her brunette hair flying in a wild disarray. She began pacing, nervously fingering the marriage license. Finally coming to a halt, she spun and faced Fargo.

"Mr. Carstairs handled the arrangements for my parents when they died. That's not my worry." She hardened even more as she added, "I want Mr. Carstairs to bury the three men—and Schatten—after they've been hanged for killing 'Rone!"

Fargo studied the woman's determined face and had a feeling she would take the law into her own hands if he did not agree to do what he could to bring her fiancé's killers to justice. And he did have a couple of leads. There had to be footprints at the edge of the courthouse, and the men must have worked for Lester Schatten.

"All right," Fargo heard himself saying, as if he were listening from a thousand miles away, hearing only echoes. Lydia came to him quickly, threw her arms around him and pulled him close. Then she kissed him on the lips. For a moment it was a thank-you. Then it became more passionate.

Fargo gently disengaged her, not wanting to take advantage of her grief.

"I'll let you know when I find out something," he said.

"You won't be disappointed," Lydia promised. And somehow Fargo doubted he would be.

Fargo got on his hands and knees as he examined the area at the side of the courthouse. The sun was setting, and it cast a bloody red tint to the ground. Every inch of ground he searched reminded him of 'Rone Clawson being shot in the back. The anger sharpened Fargo's senses and sent his brain spinning. He found three sets of boot prints and followed those belonging to the man who had remained afoot.

A few passersby gave him curious looks, but Fargo ignored them as he identified the nicks and notches on his quarry's boot soles. Although the man had run across a grassy area and emerged where dozens of others had passed, Fargo kept on the trail as it led around the far side of the courthouse back in the direction where 'Rone had tethered his horse.

Fargo heaved a sigh. The killer and thief had ridden off slowly, so as not to attract attention—other than Fargo's. The theft had been done well, so that Fargo never got a look at the man's face. The red plaid shirt he had worn was like others worn by men on the street, but it was about the only clue Fargo had to go on. He had never gotten a look at the man's face.

He rode along the street, alert for 'Rone's horse or the man who had stolen it. Fargo estimated which crossing street the thief must have taken, but saw nothing unusual down it.

"Pardon me," he called to a pedestrian. "Is there a livery anywhere near?" Fargo hoped the thief had ridden directly to a stable to sell 'Rone's horse, but knew it was as likely the man had hightailed it out of the city. He found it hard to believe three men would kill 'Rone only to steal his horse, but he had heard of stranger things. Lydia might be right that Schatten had a hand in the killing. But why steal 'Rone's horse? A bonus?

"There's one a quarter mile ahead, mister," came the answer.

"Much obliged." Fargo found the livery without any trouble. He dismounted and went inside, knowing this was likely a wild-goose chase. When this lead petered out, he would go after Lester Schatten. But first things first.

"Howdy," called out a man from inside the tack room. "Be right with you."

Fargo looked the place over. It was ill kept, almost an affront to the rest of Great Salt Lake City's cleanliness. The few horses stabled here kicked at their stalls. Fargo saw they had not been watered and doubted they had eaten recently from their gaunt sides and wild, white-rimmed

19

eyes. But there was one exception, and it made Fargo's heart leap. The horse at the rear of the livery belonged to 'Rone Clawson.

"What can I do for you?" the man asked, his beady eyes darting around as if he suspected something ill of Fargo. Stripped to the waist, the stabler sweat rivers. He was shorter than Fargo by a couple of inches, and his appearance matched those of the horses. He had been ridden hard and put away wet.

"I'm looking for the man who came in earlier today on that horse." Fargo pointed to 'Rone's horse.

"That's a new horse," the man said, his eyes darting around. "Don't know who it belongs to."

"You often stable horses without knowing the owner's name?"

"You aren't a lawman," the man said, his eyes narrowing. "What's your big interest in my customers?"

"That horse belonged to the man who was shot this afternoon."

"What killing?" the man asked, obviously lying.

"A friend of mine. Didn't say he was killed, just shot in the back."

"My mistake."

"Yeah," Fargo said. "I'd take it as a favor if you could tell me about the man who left that horse. He gunned down my partner, then stole the horse."

"Well, lemme see," the liveryman said, wiping his hands on his pants. "Joseph Benson rode out. He's an elder in the church. Then there was Miz Smith and her brood. Six of 'em, good kids, too, no matter what anyone says."

Fargo bided his time, letting the man talk. He looked around and saw the man's shirt dangling over a feed bin not five feet away. Red plaid, just like the horse thief's. Just like 'Rone's killer's.

"And then there was this one gent with the horse. Don't know his name. Came whirlin' in late this afternoon, all businesslike. Paid me in scrip on a Denver City bank to look after his horse. That very one, the one you say belongs to your partner."

"Can you describe him?"

Fargo listened to a description that might have fit half the men in Great Salt Lake City. He had not gotten a good look at the man he tracked and could not say if the stable hand was spinning him a tall tale. He thought he was.

"You say he came from Denver City?"

"Probably. Anything I can do for you, mister?"

"What happened to the tack?" Fargo saw the man start to lie, then something changed in his face. The man jerked his thumb over his shoulder in the direction of the tack room. Wary of turning his back on the man, Fargo went into the small room. 'Rone's saddle had been tossed in one corner. Checking his back before digging into the saddle-bags, Fargo looked through the contents. As far as he could tell, nothing had been taken, but everything had been dumped out and stuffed back in willy-nilly.

"Don't know if I ought to let you paw through that, mister," the liveryman said.

"Did the man who brought this in take anything with him?"

"No."

The bitterness of the answer caused Fargo to stiffen.

"Reckon I'd better tell Marshal Gutherie about this. If the man comes back, find out as much as you can about him. His name, where he's staying, anything that might help the marshal."

"All right," the liveryman said. He reached for his shirt, then edged away from it, as if realizing Fargo might recognize it as belonging to 'Rone's killer. "Not much I can do more 'n that, it bein' my civic duty."

"Mind if I look at the scrip the man paid you with?" Fargo almost laughed when the liveryman's mouth opened and snapped shut. The stable hand swallowed hard and his eyes darted around as he sought a new lie.

"Spent it already. Paid for some grain with it."

"Don't worry about it," Fargo said. "It wasn't important."

"You gonna stay around to see if he returns?"

"No, I've got to report back to the marshal," Fargo said. This seemed to be the first thing he had said to ease the liveryman's mind.

"Good luck, and I'll keep my eyes peeled," the man said, turning back to his work, or from what Fargo could tell, his avid pursuit of avoiding work. Fargo left the livery stable but did not go far. He crossed the street and watched, waiting to see if he had flushed his quarry.

He didn't have long to wait until the stable hand came hurrying out, leading 'Rone's horse. The man looked around furtively, then rode down the alley behind the livery. Fargo followed.

Fargo saw how different Great Salt Lake City was from other towns. Elsewhere the man he trailed would have ducked into a saloon or whorehouse. If such things really existed in this Mormon town, they certainly were well hidden. The man hurried along, leading Fargo through the business area of town to the edge of the city, where some fine-looking homes had been constructed.

The man might have been alert for anyone on his trail, or Fargo might have grown careless by underestimating his quarry. Whatever it was, he stopped suddenly, looked back, and spotted Fargo. Then he galloped off.

The liveryman was probably one of 'Rone's killers, and Fargo dared not lose him. This lent speed to Fargo's pursuit as he rode after him. Fargo's haste might have proven costly, as he never thought the man might take it into his head to kill another today.

The bullet cut through the brim of Fargo's hat, sending it sailing into the air. Fargo reacted reflexively, spun around in the saddle and fell hard to the ground. For a second he wondered if he ought to scramble for cover, or if the gathering twilight could hide the fact that he was unhurt.

Lying still afforded Fargo his best chance, because his reading of the man's nature told him curiosity or just plain viciousness would bring him out of hiding to look at his murderous handiwork.

It did.

Fargo heard the footsteps approaching, timidly at first, then with growing bravado as the man thought his ambush had been successful. Only when he stood a few feet away did Fargo stir.

"Son of a bitch! He's still alive!"

Fargo swept into action before the liveryman could finish the sentence. He kicked out and caught the man on his knee. A sick crunching sound echoed through the growing nighttime stillness, followed by the man's stream of profanity at the pain. Although Fargo did not bring the man to the ground, he did force him to lower the six-shooter he carried.

This let Fargo get to his feet. He towered over the man.

"Don't try lifting that hogleg," Fargo said coldly. "You missed the first time. It's my turn—and I never miss."

"You ain't even got your gun out," the man said, wincing in pain at his busted knee.

"Why did you kill 'Rone Clawson?"

"Go to hell!"

Fargo went for his six-gun instead. Both men's pistols blazed at the same instant, but Fargo's aim was better. The slug from his Colt caught the man in the chest, driving him back. When his game leg gave out under him, the stableman crashed to the ground and lay on his back, gasping for air.

His round had missed Fargo by a country mile.

"You're done for. You might as well confess what you and your partners did."

"Won't do no good," the man gasped out. Blood trickled from the hole in the middle of his chest. He raised his head and stared at it in fascination as his life's blood trickled out.

"It'll lighten your soul," Fargo said.

The man spat angrily. "I ain't no Mormon. They—" He grunted as pain racked his body. Fargo's bullet had punctured a lung, making breathing both difficult and painful.

"Who were the two with you?"

"It hurts bad, mister. You shouldna shot me like that."

Fargo stared at him, wondering how long the man had. Pink froth flecked his lips. It wouldn't be much longer before the man drowned in his own blood.

"Who pulled the trigger? The man with the rifle?"

"Gus, Gus Lamont. And the other one's even worse. He . . . he calls himself the Utah Kid."

"The Utah Kid and Gus Lamont," Fargo said, etching their names in his memory. "They did the killing, but who paid them?"

"You don't know, do you?" The man spat blood now and rolled onto his side to keep from choking.

Fargo again underestimated his enemy. He moved around to better hear the man's confession when he realized the six-shooter was no longer held in a limp hand. The man mustered all his strength to raise the heavy pistol and point it at Fargo. A trembling finger drew back on the trigger.

"See you in hell," the man said.

Again Fargo proved faster. He fired a split second before the man squeezed off his shot. Fargo's bullet ripped through the gunman's right forearm, sending his shot wild. Hot lead sang past Fargo's head again—flying harmlessly into the cool night.

He kicked the six-shooter from the man's nerveless hand and knelt to see what more he could get from him. It took Fargo only an instant to figure out the answer.

He wasn't going to learn any more from this murdering owlhoot. He was dead.

4

"Gus? Gus Lamont? Sure, I know the consarned varmint," the clerk at the supply store nearest the courthouse said to Fargo. "He waltzed out of here owing me danged near twenty dollars. Him and that worthless varmit that rides with him."

"The Utah Kid?" Fargo asked.

"That's the one. I see you already know him. Don't turn your back on him, mister. He's a mean one. As soon shoot you as look at you."

"They don't seem the type to go around on their own," Fargo said. "You hear of them working for someone? Somebody in Great Salt Lake City?"

"Rumors, nothing more. Now, you wantin' to buy or you just wantin' to talk?"

"Buy," Fargo said, getting enough supplies to keep him on the trail for a couple of weeks. It about tapped him out. All the money he had earned scouting and mapping for Captain Simpson went into beans and jerky for the hunt, but he thought it was worthwhile. He owed it to 'Rone's memory to bring the last two of his killers to justice.

And maybe unravel the thread back a bit further until he found who had paid the murderers.

"Figure Lester Schatten knows where they are?" Fargo asked, taking a shot at what the clerk had already declared in a roundabout fashion.

"If that man said up, you better look down," was all the reply he got from the clerk, who bustled off to help a portly woman with her groceries, so he could close up his store for the night. Fargo finished packing his paltry supplies into saddlebags, then left. He felt confident he knew the players in the game. Why Schatten had wanted 'Rone Clawson dead was another matter.

The two had a history. That much was obvious from the way they had clashed prior to Gus Lamont putting a rifle bullet into 'Rone's back.

Fargo considered rousting Schatten and seeing if the politician might give him some hint where his two henchmen hid out. It had not taken much digging to find that the man from the stable, who had almost parted Fargo's hair with a bullet, had been heading toward Schatten's house. As Marshal Gutherie pointed out, though, Fargo had no evidence to prove whether the man was going to Schatten's or was simply walking past.

Fargo wondered how much Schatten paid the marshal to keep him hidden away in his office and not tending to serious law enforcement.

The two killers had ridden north when they left the courthouse. Fargo knew they might have followed the road a ways, then gone in some other direction. For all he knew as fact, the dead stable hand might have been telling the truth when he said they were headed for Denver City. But Fargo doubted it. The man knew where his cohorts had gone and had dropped Colorado out as a red herring.

"That was a false trail, so what's the real one?" he mused, coming to a crossroads north of Great Salt Lake City. Fargo looked east, then he looked west and decided. He turned the Ovaro westerly, a half-moon giving enough light for him to ride at a steady pace. It wasn't until he had gone several miles that Fargo began hunting for spoor in earnest.

Any traveler along this road might have left the tracks he studied so carefully. Some wind had erased the sharpness of the hoofprints and the trail was a good six hours old now. But he had a good feeling about the two sets of prints he followed. That feeling grew when he scented a juniper-fed campfire not a hundred feet off the main road. Two men were huddled around the fire, fortunately neither had seen him.

Fargo dismounted and approached the camp using every bit of skill he had learned throughout his years in the wilderness. He dropped to his belly not ten feet from the two men and studied their faces in the flickering firelight. He was keyed up and ready to jump out at them with his Colt leveled.

Instead, he stayed where he was, hidden by undergrowth and the night.

Fargo could not positively identify the two men. They were about the right size, but he had not gotten good looks at their faces. Too much had been happening all at once for him to notice them until they had turned tail and run. He wanted to shout out their names to see if they responded, but that was no sure way to identify them, either.

Men got jumpy when strangers yelled anything, much less their names. If Fargo walked up boldly, there was no telling whether the men would give him their names—or just open fire.

He strained to overhear what they discussed in low tones, hoping to catch a name. If either so much as said 'Rone's name, Fargo would boil out of the shadows, six-shooter blazing.

Neither said anything about the killing in Great Salt Lake City, or Lester Schatten, or even called the other by name. They lied about women they had bedded and poker games they had won. After half an hour of eavesdropping, Fargo backed off quiet as a ghost and led his Ovaro to where he could make his own camp for the night.

He fell into a troubled sleep, thinking of 'Rone and Lydia and Schatten—and the man he had shot back in Great Salt Lake City.

Fargo came awake with a start as the sun poked pearly fingers over the eastern horizon. It seemed to him all of Utah sat in the bottom of a bowl, the tall mountains forming the rocky sides. He stretched, grabbed a hunk of jerky for breakfast, took a swig of water, then set out after the two men. He felt they were 'Rone's killers, but he had to be sure before taking them in. Not only would he make a pair of enemies if he was wrong, he would have wasted precious time that could have otherwise been used hunting the real Gus Lamont and the Utah Kid.

Time was something he dared not fritter away or the trail would grow cold and the killers would simply vanish.

He waited patiently for the two men to finish their breakfast and come riding out onto the main road. They looked as taciturn as they had been the night before, exchanging a few words and then lapsing into long silences. Fargo let them get a fifteen-minute head start, then rode after them, turning over plan after plan in his mind.

He was a good hunter, some said the best. The Trailsman seldom lost his quarry, and was not about to do so now while hunting two men. But the best way of approaching them was a poser. Sometimes stealthy tracking worked, other times the bold approach was best.

Fargo rode just fast enough to overtake the men within a half hour of them leaving their camp. The taller of the pair, the one with the ugly scar across his forehead, turned and studied Fargo for a few seconds, then turned back and spoke to his partner.

Fargo was close enough to see his squinty eyes and feel the coldness in his gaze. He had a sharp nose and sunken cheeks, as if he had been starved for a spell.

"Howdy!" he called as he rode up. "You're the first pilgrims I've seen since leaving Great Salt Lake City. Where you heading?"

"You're mighty nosy," the hatchet-faced man said. Fargo saw the way the man rode with his hand near the butt of his six-shooter, as if he would throw down on Fargo in a heartbeat. If Fargo had been a betting man, he would have laid his money down that this was the Utah Kid.

"You're mighty unfriendly," Fargo said, riding even with them. "You got something to hide?"

"Why'd you say that?" demanded the other man, the one Fargo figured to be Gus Lamont—making him the man who had pulled the trigger, killing 'Rone Clawson.

"From the way your friend acts," Fargo said. "Didn't mean to rile you. I was just being friendly." He gave them hard looks and urged his Ovaro to more speed.

"Wait!" called Lamont, after hasty words with his partner. "Don't go ridin' off like that."

"Why? Should I stick around so you can insult me? You act like I'm the law."

"Is that a fact?" asked the Utah Kid. "Why would you go and say a thing like that? You sayin' we're on the lam?"

"You've got the look of someone who's ridden the outlaw trail," Fargo allowed. "Truth is, you look like a right famous gunfighter named the Utah Kid. But you couldn't be him."

"What? Why not?" Fargo held back a grin, as the kid's reaction couldn't have been scripted any better.

"Gossip has it he is a stone killer, a real gunman. You're just some cowpoke out hunting for another job with some cattle spread."

"You think so? Well, let me tell you, I *am* the Utah Kid!"

"No!" Fargo feigned surprise. "That would mean you're his partner, Gus Lamont. Why, you two are famous!"

The two outlaws exchanged glances and a silent communication flowed between them that Fargo read easily. Before the Utah Kid could clear leather, Fargo had his Colt out and swinging hard. The barrel caught the Kid alongside the head and knocked him from the saddle. He hit the ground hard and lay still.

"Damned lawman!" cried Lamont. Gus saw what had happened to his partner but chose to run rather than fight. For that Fargo thanked his lucky stars. If Lamont had drawn, he might have gotten a shot off—into Fargo's gut.

Instead, he put his heels to his horse's sides and galloped off. Fargo shot a quick glance back at the Utah Kid still motionless on the ground, then started after Gus Lamont. The Ovaro was a stronger horse, and Lamont was not trying to conserve the strength of his mount. Yard by yard Fargo overtook the fleeing outlaw.

Lamont looked over his shoulder and saw Fargo nearing. He tried to veer off the road and head for rougher country in an attempt to lose Fargo, but his horse stepped in a prairie-dog hole. The leg of Lamont's horse broke with a gruesome snap.

Fargo reined back hard when he saw Lamont flying head over heels through the air to land on the ground. The man groaned, but Fargo's attention went to his horse. The poor animal neighed loudly and tried to stand on its broken leg.

Without hesitation, Fargo drew his Henry from its saddle sheath, levered a round into the chamber, and fired. The bullet put the horse out of its misery. Then he turned to the man who had murdered 'Rone Clawson.

"Wait, no, don't!" cried Gus Lamont, on his knees as if praying. "You can't shoot me down like a dog."

"You're right," Fargo said. "That would be a waste of good ammunition."

Seeing the smirk on Lamont's face, Fargo levered a new round in and said, "On the other hand, turning you into buzzard bait would be awfully satisfying, seeing how you shot my partner in the back."

"He was your partner? I didn't know that. Hell, I didn't even know his name."

"You murdered a man without even having a grudge against him?" Fargo lifted the Henry and sighted along the octagonal gunmetal-blue barrel, centering the forward bead squarely in the notch so it rested on Lamont's face.

"Wait, it wasn't my fault. He told us to do it. He *paid* us. I couldn't pass up fifty dollars, could you?"

"Fifty dollars? That's what a man's life is worth?" Anger creeped into his voice.

"You don't want to kill me," Lamont pleaded.

"Who paid you?" Fargo asked louder this time.

"He'd be real mad if—" Lamont went pale when Fargo made a point of pulling back the rifle hammer. The distinctive click must have sounded like the peal of doom to Lamont.

"Who paid you?" repeated Fargo. He almost wished Lamont would keep his foul mouth shut so he could justify shooting the man down, but the Trailsman would never kill a man in cold blood, no matter how much he deserved it. He would take Lamont back alive to Great Salt Lake City for trial, but the backshooter didn't need to know that.

"It was Schatten." Lamont blubbered. "Lester Schatten!"

"You willing to say that in court?"

"Court? They'll *hang* me!"

"Not if you tell the judge what you just told me. He'll probably send you to the territorial prison rather than stretching your miserable neck."

"I'll spill everything. I'll swear that Schatten was the one who paid us."

Fargo lowered the rifle, unsatisfied with the way this had gone. For him, and he suspected for Lydia Pressman as well, justice would not be served by just sending the man who had pulled the trigger to prison. But if Lamont and the Utah Kid testified against Schatten, that might be good enough.

He doubted it, but unless he was willing to shoot down

a man in cold blood, Fargo had no other choice. Fortunately for Lester Schatten that wasn't the way he did things.

He got Lamont walking back toward Great Salt Lake City. Along the way, they found the Utah Kid, still shaken and head hurting from the buffaloing Fargo had given him. Fargo rode his Ovaro and forced the two killers to walk. It was little enough punishment for them until he could turn them over to Marshal Guthcrie.

5

"It's enough to make a body think there still can be miracles worked on earth," Lydia Pressman said. "You found 'Rone's killers within a day of him, of him . . . passing on."

"He was murdered," Fargo said, harsher than he intended. Lydia might be glad Lamont and the Utah Kid were in custody awaiting trial, but he wanted Schatten behind bars, as well. More than that, he wanted to know that justice would be done, and Schatten would have his neck stretched on the gallows.

"I know, Skye, I know." Lydia turned her lovely brown eyes on him. They shone with an intense inner light as she studied him head to toe and back up again. The way she smiled told him she liked what she saw. A lot. "Everyone's always good to me, but you've been especially kind, bringing back 'Rone's horse and belongings."

"Did you have a chance to go through his things to see if anything was stolen?"

"I . . . I didn't find anything. I mean, I don't think anything was taken, but there's not much there to remember a man like 'Rone by."

From the condition of the saddlebags' contents, Fargo thought the stable hand had already rifled through 'Rone's possessions. It was good that nothing had been taken, that Lydia had everything back and that he had done what he could. But Fargo felt there was something more, something he was missing.

"I know you did it because you were 'Rone's partner, and he was lucky to know a man like you, but I feel all your efforts have been for me." She batted her long eyelashes in his direction, then moved closer to sit beside him. The day was warm; Lydia's thigh pressing against his was warmer.

Fargo had seen seductive women in his day, but none held a candle to Lydia Pressman—and none had ever seemed so hot for him.

"I did it for you," Fargo said. "For you and 'Rone and me."

"I suppose so," Lydia said, heaving a deep sigh. She turned just enough so he could see the way her breasts rose and fell with every breath. Fargo had seen bait put out before, but never anything this delectable. He wondered why she was so intent on catching him. Lydia was an attractive woman, but she had been his partner's intended.

Fargo licked his lips even as he considered that 'Rone had been his partner and Lydia was free to do as she chose now.

"I'll be going now, Lydia," he said.

"You won't stay for the funeral?" She seemed upset he was leaving.

"I never cared much for them, maybe because I've seen so many."

"I understand," she said, surprising him with her empathy. It was as if she looked into his heart and soul and knew the pain there. Maybe their shared pain over losing 'Rone gave her such insight. Lydia stood and held out her hands. He took them in his and wondered if he ought to kiss her. She looked as if she expected it, but Fargo did not trust himself. One kiss would be too many—and not enough.

Suddenly, the glass in the front window exploded inward. Fargo reacted without thinking. He dived forward and wrapped Lydia in his arms, carrying her to the floor. The woman struggled under him.

"Hush," he said, rolling off her. He came to his feet with his six-shooter ready for action. Using the barrel, Fargo moved aside the curtain on the window that had been shot out. Fargo pieced it all together. He had heard a gunshot and the breaking glass at about the same instant, meaning the shooter was close to the house. As he peered out the broken window, Fargo saw what he had expected.

Lester Schatten jammed a six-gun back into his belt and rushed off, not running but walking at a less-than-comfortable pace.

"Who did it?" asked Lydia, coming up close behind Fargo.

"Schatten. He must have heard Lamont and the Utah Kid were in jail."

"Why shoot at me?" She sounded outraged rather than frightened.

Fargo considered the answer carefully. Schatten might not have been shooting at Lydia. Getting rid of the man who might be responsible for him standing trial for murder was a powerful motive for trying to ambush Fargo. Or perhaps the crooked politician played a deeper game. This might have been intended as a warning for him to get out of town, or Lydia Pressman's life would be forfeit.

Schatten did not know the Trailsman if he thought such threats would work. If anything, they firmed Fargo's resolve in seeing the politician dangle from a rope around his neck. He started for the door.

"Don't, Skye, please," Lydia said when Fargo started after the escaping politician. "Don't leave me."

"I can catch him," protested Fargo.

"We know he did it. This is nothing compared to how he ordered 'Rone murdered. Let it go."

"I want him in jail with Lamont and the Kid."

"Don't go. Stay with me. I need you, Skye."

Lydia clung to him tightly. Fargo knew he ought to go after Schatten, but he felt himself responding to the woman's nearness. She felt it, too. A ghost of a smile flickered across her ruby lips. Her hand moved restlessly over his back and then slid between them, moving down to his crotch.

"That must be painful," she said. "We ought to do something about it."

"This isn't right. 'Rone's not even buried yet."

"It's right, Skye. I need to know everything will go on, that everything will be fine without 'Rone." She turned her face up to his. Her chocolate-brown eyes glistened, but not with tears. They shone with excitement and lust. "If 'Rone hadn't come along first and I'd seen you, I'd have fallen for you, Skye. You're so big . . ."

Fargo swallowed when the woman began squeezing rhythmically at his crotch. He was growing harder and resisting Lydia's allure was almost impossible. She was excited to be with him and did everything she could to spur him on, with sexy looks and seductive touches. Fargo put an index finger under her chin and lifted her face to his so he could kiss her slightly parted lips.

The kiss started out gentle and became increasingly passionate. Fargo felt Lydia's body crush into his. Her breasts rubbed against his chest, and her hand never let up the gentle massaging that excited him so much.

When her tongue boldly snaked out to engage his, Fargo knew he was lost. It no longer seemed wrong to have such feelings for his dead partner's fiancée. Instead, nothing had ever seemed more right to him. She fit nicely into the circle of his arms, and her sweet mouth was like heady summer wine. Pushing his arousal ever higher was her darting tongue running all over his. The kiss deepened and excited Fargo to the point he could hardly endure the pressure within his loins.

"I want more," he said.

"Take it," she responded in a husky whisper. "Anything, everything you want. I'm all yours!"

Fargo bent and scooped the woman up in a smooth movement. He held her close and their mouths remained locked as he carried her into the small bedroom. The four-poster bed creaked as he gently laid her down before him. She twisted around, her skirts hiked as she stared wantonly at him. She saw where his eyes wandered and teased him by lifting those billowy skirts ever higher, inch by slow, tormenting inch.

"See what you want?" she asked softly.

"Yes!"

He placed his hands on the insides of her legs and slowly followed the hem of her skirts up as Lydia pulled the unwanted garment away from her body. Fargo's hands slid over silky-smooth flesh, reaching her thighs. Once there he could not restrain himself. He bent and lavished wet kisses on her tender flesh. Lydia fell back weakly on the bed, moaning with pleasure.

Fargo drew down Lydia's frilly undergarments, exposing a dew-dropped fleecy brunette bush nestled between her legs. Kissing her legs and moving closer to the center of her sensation drove the woman wild with need. She thrashed about on the bed, her legs lifted on either side of Fargo's head.

When he ran his finger along her molten center, she lifted herself off the bed, arched her back, and began grinding against his hand. Fargo wiggled his finger about in her heated core until she let out a cry of ultimate release and sank down to the bed.

"I . . . I've never felt like that before," she gasped out. "I still feel all tingly—"

Fargo freed himself from his gun belt and boots, then skinned out of his jeans. He saw the expression on Lydia's face and knew there was no way he could stop himself now. She wanted him as badly as he wanted her.

"More, Skye, give me more of you," she cried. Lydia sat up and stripped off her now-wrinkled blouse to expose the twin cones of creamy flesh he had only imagined before. The sleek slopes were capped with the bright red cherries of her nipples. Fargo dropped to the bed and sucked one into his mouth. When he pressed his tongue against it hard, he felt the frenzied beating of Lydia's heart.

He nibbled and gnawed on one breast and then slipped down her milky slope and spiraled back up to give the same oral treatment to the other breast and the nipple capping it. As his mouth worked avidly on the scrumptious feast she provided for him, he stroked his finger in and out of her tight recess. He held her captive between finger and mouth—and every instant made him ache with need that much more.

Lydia arched her back again, driving her groin hard into his hand. He felt a flood of slick juices and heard her cries of desire as new waves of ecstasy washed through her lush body.

"More," she panted. "More. I want you inside me, Skye."

She reached down and fumbled a mite as she gripped his hardness. The brunette tugged gently to get him between her wantonly widespread legs. He positioned himself, and she guided him to the target that they both desired hit.

Fargo grunted as he felt her tightness around his organ. He almost got off like a young buck with his first piece of tail. He shoved his hips forward and sank another inch into paradise. Her inner walls were hot, wet, and tight. Surrounding him. Clutching at him.

He levered himself forward a tad more and sank deep into her clinging moist center. Fargo looked down at Lydia's face. Her eyes were screwed shut, and she tossed her head from side to side as the feverish pitch built within her again.

He rotated his hips slightly, stirring himself around in her depths like a spoon in a mixing bowl. Then he pulled back slowly, tormenting her with every inch. When only the heavy tip of his rod remained hidden between her nether lips, he slammed forward with all the speed and desire locked up within him, lifting Lydia off the bed again.

She cried out in delight and began grinding herself against him. He joined in, moving in the direction opposite hers to give them both the maximum pleasure possible. He withdrew slowly, then rammed back in harder and faster. Teasing her, tormenting her, he built up his own tensions until they reached the breaking point. Deep within he felt the white-hot tide rising. By now his rhythm had changed, turned ragged, filling him with urgent need.

Wildly, he drove in and out of her. The friction of his manhood against her clutching female sheath burned brightly for both of them. He could no longer deny the inexorable tide of heat rising in him. He tried to split her apart with his steely hardness as he exploded.

Lydia moaned, sobbed and clung fiercely to him as she hunched up. Locked together, they rolled over on the bed, then rolled again and came to rest. Fargo was spent but remained hidden away in the softness of Lydia's inner reaches.

She giggled as she stroked over his sweaty face with her trembling fingers. "You're melting," she said.

"Got good reason," Fargo said, pulling her closer. Her breasts were as firm and thrilling as ever, but now there was nothing he could do about it. Limply slipping from her, he was no longer good for anything.

Or so he thought. Lydia's mouth knew tricks unlike any Fargo could recall, and before he knew it they were again making love in the warm Great Salt Lake City afternoon.

* * *

Fargo's mind wandered during 'Rone Clawson's funeral. Lydia stood next to him, wrapped up in her widow's weeds and private thoughts. The words were pretty and ought to have put any man's—or woman's—heart to rest about Moroni Clawson's eventual destination in death, but Fargo found himself looking around for signs of Lester Schatten.

The politician had made himself scarce since shooting out Lydia's window. From what Marshal Gutherie said, Schatten was nowhere to be found. Fargo doubted the marshal had put forth too much of an effort, suspecting the lawman to be beholden to Schatten. But others knew what had happened and how Lamont and the Utah Kid had both declared Schatten to be the one who hired him to kill 'Rone. Gutherie might not want to find Schatten, but the citizens of Great Salt Lake City would. This was a peaceable, law-abiding town, and they would keep it that way.

"Do you wish to say anything, Mr. Fargo?"

It took Fargo a second to realize the Mormon minister was talking to him. He shook his head.

"There's nothing I can say that you haven't already. 'Rone was a good man."

The ceremony finished quickly, leaving Lydia and Fargo beside the coffin at the open grave. Behind them stood the undertaker and two men with shovels, prepared to begin the chore of replacing the dirt they had just dug.

"I thought I wouldn't cry," Lydia said, mopping at the tears running down her cheeks. "I was wrong."

"You'll be fine. It'll take time, but you're a strong woman."

"And I have such good friends to help me through my grief," she said, smiling a bit and showing some of the spirit that had drawn Fargo to her originally. She clung to his arm for support. It still bothered him how he had helped her get over some of her sorrow before the funeral, but maybe that was as much a needed medicine as anything she might have gotten from a doctor.

"Go on. I'll see to the undertaker," Fargo said, indicating Carstairs and the men with him. The cost of the funeral wore on him because he didn't have much money left after outfitting himself to go after Lamont and the Utah Kid. Then it hit him that 'Rone had almost twenty dollars on him when he'd been killed. He had only spent a dollar for the marriage license. Otherwise, his pay from their mapping and scouting work at Camp Floyd was intact. That ought to cover most all the expenses of planting him in this fancy cemetery and giving him a decent marker.

Carstairs watched Lydia make her way to the buggy and waited for Fargo.

"You taking care of the expenses for the lady?" he asked.

"Reckon so. How much is it?"

"Coffin, burial detail, other arrangements, twenty dollars," Carstairs said.

That struck Fargo as being a bit steep, but he was not going to barter over a dead man's last rites.

Fargo reached into his pocket and pulled out a silver coin. He tossed it to the undertaker and closed out 'Rone Clawson's last tab. "He had nineteen on him when he was killed. Keep it."

"All right. I'll do that," Carstairs said too quickly. He almost looked as if he was going to bolt and run. Fargo looked at the man, wondering what the problem might be. Carstairs nervously wiped his lips, showing a flashy gold ring. When he saw Fargo staring at him, he jerked his hand away, shoved it into his coat pocket and shouted to his men to start working.

He pushed past Fargo and joined the two men shoveling dirt onto 'Rone's coffin. Something about Carstairs bothered Fargo, but he could not put it into words. All the way back to Lydia's house, the undertaker's strange behavior gnawed at him.

"I'll be going, Lydia," he told her.

"Stay the night, Skye. I enjoyed this afternoon immensely, but tonight I just want someone with me to hold me, to be near." Her voice was as compelling as a Siren's.

"A mighty attractive offer," he said, "and one I'm not inclined to turn down. But I have to. I've got some business to tend to. I'll look in on you tomorrow morning, if that's all right."

"It is," Lydia said. A weak smile danced on her lips, then she turned and walked into her house. Fargo felt like a traitor, denying her the way he had. She did not seem to have anyone else coming over to stay with her, but it was getting dark and perhaps her friends had their own concerns to tend to.

Fargo saddled his Ovaro and mounted, his mind racing. He disliked funerals, and this one had been especially hard for him. 'Rone had been his partner and Lydia was his partner's woman. More than that, something bothered him about the way Carstairs had responded when they had talked about the cost of the funeral.

"The ring," Fargo said to himself. "The ring Carstairs wore! That was 'Rone's ring!"

Fargo had been with Lydia all day and the undertaker had not delivered any of the dead man's belongings, such as they were. While Carstairs might have sent the possessions to another relative, Fargo couldn't remember 'Rone mentioning anyone. As far as he knew, 'Rone had been alone in the world, except for his betrothed. The rest of his family, like Lydia's, had died from a variety of common ailments and accidents. When Fargo had told Carstairs to keep the money 'Rone had carried, it had spooked the undertaker. Fargo guessed the reason was that Carstairs had already taken that money for his own, along with 'Rone's ring.

What else had the undertaken taken?

Fargo rode back to the cemetery to find out, as disagreeable as he knew it might prove to be.

6

Fargo's hands ached from shoveling the dirt off 'Rone's grave, and he hated the idea of disturbing his partner's eternal rest. The funeral had been good enough for any man and ought to have sent 'Rone off to the promised land in style. To open the grave again within hours of the burial was a corruption of faith.

But Fargo had to do it. He owed it to 'Rone—and to Lydia—to be sure of his suspicions before he accused the undertaker of anything as vile as robbing the dead.

He heaved one last shovel of dirt out of the grave, leaving the coffin exposed. Fargo dropped to his knees and pryed open the lid. The sudden release of gases from inside gagged Fargo. He had not expected such an odor to build this fast. Keeping his gorge down, he peered into the coffin at his friend.

Fargo blinked in surprise. He had seen Lydia lay out fine duds for 'Rone to be buried in, but now the man was naked. The ring that had caught Fargo's attention when they first met almost a year back was gone from the hand laid across the chest. He did not need to look further to know anything that had been 'Rone's before he was interred was now gone.

"Stolen by that son of a bitch Carstairs," Fargo muttered. He brushed the dirt from his hands and crawled from the grave, sitting on the edge and staring at his partner's naked corpse. Fargo had no idea what to do next. Going to Marshal Gutherie without evidence of Carstairs's responsibility was a waste of time. He had seen how the lawman had tried to push aside doing his duty in favor of keeping things exactly the way they were.

More than this, Carstairs might be innocent. There had

been two helpers with him to dig the grave, and the undertaker might have innocently accepted 'Rone's ring from one of them. Either of the laborers might have robbed 'Rone of everything with him in the coffin. There might even be an assistant in the funeral parlor entrusted with preparing the bodies who was responsible.

Fargo sucked in some of the cool night air laced with salt from the nearby Great Salt Lake, then jumped back into the grave to replace the coffin lid and begin the tedious chore of shoveling the dirt back over 'Rone Clawson. As he sealed the grave, he also sealed his lips. Whatever evidence he obtained against the undertaker had to be independent of what had been done to 'Rone. Fargo wanted to protect Lydia from even more pain.

Tamping the last of the dirt in a mound over his partner, Fargo got on his horse and rode in the direction of the funeral parlor. It was late, with dawn only an hour off, but Fargo thought he might break into the undertaker's and see what he could find in the way of evidence.

He rode through the deserted streets until he neared the funeral parlor. Fargo hastily dismounted and ducked down an alley by the mortuary. A wagon had come to a halt in front of the building. A manlike shape covered with a tarp lay in the back.

A loud knock on the door brought an almost immediate response. To Fargo's surprise, Carstairs was already at work.

"Got another one for you, Mr. Carstairs," the wagon driver said. "The marshal found him outside town. Looks to have died from foul play."

"How do you mean?" asked Carstairs.

"Might have been hit on the head and knocked into a ditch."

"Hit and run?" asked Carstairs. "Who would not stop to aid a man injured in this fashion?"

"Can't say. I just pick 'em up when the marshal asks. You want the stiff taken round back?"

"Yes, yes, I was finishing another . . . client. There is room for one more. Will this be a pauper's funeral?"

"Reckon so. Can't tell who this is or if he's got relatives or friends willing to foot the bill."

"Any identification would be helpful," Carstairs said in

his precise, prissy fashion. Fargo peered around the corner of the building to where the driver shifted nervously from foot to foot while the undertaker persisted.

"Look, I just pick 'em up, I don't search 'em. That'd be wrong."

"Yes, of course. Do bring the deceased to the rear." Carstairs closed the door, letting the driver jump into the box and get his team rattling around the block. Fargo ducked back down the alley where he had watched, and looked around the rear of the building.

Before the driver could leap down from the box, Carstairs emerged, pushing a table on wheels.

"I will tend to the deceased," Carstairs said.

"Thanks, I appreciate that. Uh, you gonna pay me or do I have to get my money from Marshal Guthrie?"

"For the delivery?" Carstairs whipped off the canvas tarp and studied the body for a few seconds. "I will pay you, my good man. One dollar?"

"That's the going rate."

Carstairs fished in his pocket, drawing out a silver coin—a cartwheel. He passed it to the driver, then silently returned to wrestle the body onto the table. The driver snapped the reins and rattled off without a backward glance, driving past where Fargo was hidden.

Carstairs pushed the body back into the funeral parlor. Fargo hurried down the alley and caught the door before it snapped shut. He slipped into the cool, dank interior and almost gave himself away by gagging. The chemical odors overwhelmed him. Taking short, quick breaths through his mouth helped Fargo regain his composure.

From a room down the hall came melodic singing as Carstairs worked on the new corpse. Fargo walked quietly past two other small preparation rooms and peered in at Carstairs. The undertaker methodically stripped the corpse. When he got to a roll of greenbacks, Carstairs counted the money, then tucked it into a coat pocket. He fumbled a ring off the body's finger, then held it up to the light from a kerosene lamp. Like a young lady admiring a new bauble, he viewed it from all sides.

Fargo sucked in his breath when Carstairs took off 'Rone's ring, put it safely away into his pocket, then settled the newly stolen ring on his finger. The undertaker went back to work on the corpse, examining the boots before putting them into a closet alongside a half dozen other pairs.

By the time Carstairs got to the trousers, Fargo had seen enough. He had no idea what arrangement Carstairs had with Marshal Guthrie, but it was obvious the undertaker was robbing the dead. It made Fargo's gorge rise, but it was a matter for the law to deal with.

The sun poked above the horizon as Fargo got to the marshal's office, bringing a hint of desert heat to the city. It would get a lot hotter before the end of the day and Fargo knew it.

"Marshal?" Fargo walked to the lawman's desk and glared at him. Gutherie had two stacks of paper in front of him. From all Fargo could tell, the marshal moved papers from the top of one stack to the top of the other, not doing anything productive in the process.

"What can I do for you, Mr. Fargo? It's not about the Clawson killing, is it? I got those varmints securely jailed, and if I can get the district attorney moving, we'll bring charges against Mr. Schatten. I got to say, you helped clear up a passel of problems. Lamont and the Utah Kid both got wanted posters on them for robbing pilgrims over near Camp Floyd."

"Good, good," Fargo said, hardly listening. He was too occupied with what he had found out about the undertaker. "There's something else I wanted to bring to your attention." Fargo started with his suspicions and, as he talked, the marshal's face turned paler and paler. After Fargo finished Gutherie sat for a moment, speechless.

He started to say something, but no words came out. Then he settled his nerves and forced out his thoughts. "This is a mighty serious charge, Fargo. I don't know if you seeing what you say you saw is proof enough to arrest Mr. Carstairs."

"Check out the way he works for yourself."

"He's a married man, a decent one from all accounts. I never had a complaint against him, which is unusual for a man in his profession. When I worked over in Laramie, there were people griping all the time about the way the undertaker overcharged them."

"Carstairs avoids that by stealing from the dead," Fargo

44

said. He told how Carstairs had replaced Clawson's ring with one from the new body.

"This is too serious a charge for me not to investigate, but I don't know how to go about it," Gutherie admitted.

"How many bodies a day does Carstairs get for burial?"

Gutherie rubbed his stubbled chin as he thought. "A couple a week, usually. It's pretty quiet in Great Salt Lake City."

"The next one that goes to him ought to have something distinctive in a pocket or on a finger," Fargo said.

"You mean plant the evidence?"

"Put it there to see if Carstairs is honest. It'll work better if the body is of some upstanding citizen with friends and family who might want the jewelry."

Fargo turned to go when he saw the man who had delivered the body to Carstairs's funeral parlor hurry down the street toward the marshal's office. Fargo stepped back and waited. The man came into Marshal Gutherie's office and Fargo stood to one side so he could listen.

"Marshal, you know old man Hannigan? Got word he just died."

"What was he, eighty years old?"

"At least. He came with Brigham Young from Nauvoo ten years back, and he was old then. Figured you'd want to tell the elders personally, him bein' one of the original settlers and all."

Gutherie looked past the man to Fargo. From the set to the marshal's jaw, Fargo knew the lawman was not going to pass up this opportunity to unearth Carstairs's transgressions.

"John," he said to the driver, "let me tell you what we are going to do."

"That should be enough to prime the pump," Marshal Gutherie said, putting a diamond stickpin into the dead man's lapel.

"Where'd you get it?" Fargo asked. The headlight diamond shone like the sun on the inside of Joseph Hannigan's lapel. The marshal flipped the lapel over so the stone was hidden.

"Been in my family a while. Got it from my brother." Gutherie glared at Fargo, as if daring him to pursue the matter. Fargo had seen tinhorn gamblers wearing similar headlight diamonds as a way of carrying wealth and to advertise their success at faro or poker.

Fargo stepped to one side of the neat, quiet bedroom and let John and the marshal carry out the body. He nodded politely to the grieving family, wondering what Gutherie had told them. From the way they stared, he guessed it had not been much, but they had gone along with it because he was the marshal.

John rattled away in his wagon, heading for Carstairs's funeral parlor. Fargo saw the way Marshal Gutherie clenched his hands and then forced himself to relax, only to clench both fists and teeth in anger again. Something had already alerted the lawman to the truth about Carstairs. Fargo had only sealed the matter with what he had seen.

"Let's go," Gutherie said. He and Fargo mounted and rode slowly after the wagon. By the time they reached the mortuary, John had already unloaded the body at the rear door and given it over to Carstairs.

"Do we go in the front way?" Fargo asked. He saw that they were no longer alone. Three deputies waited for them outside the funeral parlor, showing how seriously Gutherie took the charges. He had not pursued Schatten this aggressively.

"In a few minutes. I want to make sure he has time to examine the body." Gutherie had turned taciturn but looked as if he would explode at any instant.

The marshal gestured to his men, sending one around to the rear to cut off any escape. Another stayed outside the front door and the other crowded in behind Fargo as they stepped into another world. The vestibule was dark, quiet, and carried a hint of perfume in the air. Tasteful paintings hung on the walls and heavy plum-colored velvet curtains draped off alcoves on either side. Ahead along a short hall opened a viewing room.

Gutherie waited impatiently for five minutes, then was unable to contain himself any longer. The marshal stalked forward, thumbs jammed into his gun belt so his hand would be closer to the butt of his Smith & Wesson. He stopped, squared his stance, and called out to Carstairs.

The undertaker came from the preparation room in the

rear, dressed in a long black cloth coat and with a sympathetic expression on his face. Fargo would have bought the act if he hadn't seen what Gutherie did right away. On Carstairs's left lapel rode the diamond stickpin that had just come in on Joseph Hannigan's body.

"You son of a bitch!" shouted Gutherie. He crossed the room and delivered a wild haymaker that landed on the side of Carstairs's head. The undertaker fell heavily. The marshal wasn't going to stop his punishment. He kicked the downed man until the deputy pulled him back.

"Don't, Marshal, he's not worth it."

The deputy held a struggling Gutherie back as Fargo reached down and plucked the stickpin from the undertaker's lapel.

"You got a powerful lot of explaining to do," Fargo said.

Carstairs looked up, but said nothing.

"Search the place. Find out if he's got anything else here. See if he has any of *her* things." The way Gutherie said it, Fargo knew the marshal meant someone special.

"Right, Marshal," said the deputy, releasing the lawman but watching for a moment to be sure Gutherie didn't start whaling away on the undertaker again.

"How could you do it, Carstairs? There wasn't anyone in Great Salt Lake City that didn't respect you," the lawman said bitterly.

"I am not sure what you mean, Marshal Gutherie," Carstairs said, straightening his coat and getting to his feet. A knot the size of a goose egg welled up where the marshal had struck him.

"You're not going to like this one bit, Marshal," called the deputy from the back room. "Come and have a look."

Fargo joined Gutherie. A half dozen wardrobes were stuffed with clothing. Drawers of money and jewelry filled an armoire. The deputy held up a cheap brooch.

"I'll kill you!" raged Gutherie, flying at Carstairs with blood in his eyes. This time Fargo got between them before the lawman could do much damage to the unresisting undertaker. The outburst brought the other two deputies on the run. One of them held Gutherie as the other began pawing through the drawers of jewelry.

"I don't believe this. He must have stolen from every last person he buried."

"Whose brooch is that?" Fargo asked quietly, pointing to the one the other deputy had found.

Stricken eyes fixed on Fargo. The deputy finally came to a decision and said, "The marshal's wife had one exactly like that. She died six months back birthin' their second son. Carstairs buried her with it. The brooch was his wedding present to her."

Fargo was sorry he had stopped Gutherie from beating the undertaker to a bloody pulp.

7

Fargo wondered if he would ever get over the desolation he felt standing at the foot of the steps leading to Lydia Pressman's front porch. Before, he had mounted those three steps to tell her that 'Rone was gone. Now he had to tell her of Carstairs's treachery and how he had robbed the dead.

"Skye, is that you?"

"Lydia," he said, mounting the steps to face her as she opened the door. "I've got some more bad news."

"What is it? Schatten?"

"No, it's 'Rone." The confusion on her face told him he had phrased it poorly. "It's about his funeral and the undertaker."

"Mr. Carstairs? I don't understand. Come in and tell me what's going on." She stepped to one side, letting Fargo enter. He brushed against her trim body and felt a thrill at the woman's nearness when her hand touched his. This was no time to get confused about why he had come.

Fargo spent the next ten minutes telling Lydia what had happened. To his surprise she took the news well. If anything, she seemed overjoyed.

"Then he lied to me?" she asked, her brown eyes wide and shining.

"What did he say?"

"That there wasn't anything on 'Rone, that all I had to do was supply some fancy clothing for him to be buried in. There *was* something on him when he was gunned down?"

"Reckon so. I noticed Carstairs wearing 'Rone's ring at the funeral."

"I do want a keepsake, but not his ring, especially if Carstairs actually wore it. I . . . I'd prefer something more personal." Her eyes shone like beacons now. "His watch," she said, choosing her words carefully, "was not with his belongings in his saddlebags. You must know what that watch meant to him. Did Carstairs take it, too?"

"I can't say. Since he showed how sticky his fingers were for everything else, I doubt he would let a gold watch go unnoticed."

"So how do I get it back?" She leaned forward and took his hand in hers. Lydia's eyes grew wide and her cheeks flushed slightly, highlighting her beauty. Fargo knew a man could be sucked down into those eyes and never surface again.

She was lovely, but Fargo wasn't sure he wanted what she was offering, except he had made a promise to a dying man to do for her. Fargo had to admit Lydia had ended up with little more than the worthless marriage license to remember 'Rone by.

"Did 'Rone ever write you any letters?" he asked.

Lydia's eyes narrowed. "Why do you ask?"

"Those might give a better remembrance," Fargo said, wondering at her suspicion. Lydia relaxed a mite but remained on guard.

"You knew 'Rone. He wasn't much for writing letters."

"Reckon not," Fargo said.

"Please, Skye, could you find me *something* to properly remember 'Rone by? Any little thing, but not his ring." Lydia studied him again, like a poker player sizing up an opponent.

"I remember how 'Rone loved that watch," Fargo said. "We'd sit around a campfire and he would spin it around on its chain. I'm not sure I ever saw him check the time, but he was always playing with the watch."

"It was a legacy from his pa, passed down to 'Rone's older brother and eventually to 'Rone. He never spoke of them much. Their deaths were painful for him." Lydia took a deep breath, causing her breasts to rise and press against her prim starched white blouse until Fargo thought the buttons might pop off. She exhaled hard and said, "Anything you do for me will be very so much appreciated, Skye. You know that. You've been *so* good to me already, I hardly know how to thank you."

"It's what I owe a partner," Fargo allowed, knowing

50

there was more to it than that. Lydia was a beautiful woman, and it got mighty lonely out in the wilderness. "Marshal Gutherie was heading to Carstairs's house to search for more evidence. If we go, you might help out by identifying 'Rone's belongings." Again Fargo was startled by how quickly Lydia moved. She shot to her feet and stood waiting for him.

Fargo drove the buggy. The whole way to Carstairs's house, the woman muttered to herself but never actually spoke, except to give directions.

"It looks like the circus has come to town," Fargo observed. A crowd had gathered around Carstairs's house. He rode through them, then went to help Lydia down from the carriage, but she had already jumped to the ground and was hurrying into the house. Fargo followed, puzzled. It was not the mien of a stricken widow—or at least a woman cruelly riven from her fiancé—but more like a prospector hot on the trail of golden treasure.

Fargo got inside as Lydia finished telling Marshal Gutherie what she expected to find, giving a decent description of 'Rone's watch. She finished saying, "Or anything else, really. I just need to remember 'Rone, like you do your beloved Julia."

Gutherie looked past her to Fargo, as if accusing him of bringing Lydia to a place where she might suffer some more. The marshal was upset how Lydia had mentioned his dead wife, bringing back an unpleasant reminder of Carstairs's crime.

"You find anything more, Marshal?" Fargo asked.

"I don't believe it. The whole house is filled with the belongings of men and women he's robbed for nigh on five years." Gutherie looked over his shoulder at a small, mousy woman sitting patiently in the corner. "Every last stitch of clothing in Mrs. Carstairs's wardrobe was taken off the dead."

"What of the jewelry? Mr. Fargo said he noticed 'Rone's ring on Carstairs's finger. What else did he take from 'Rone?"

"Please, Miss Pressman, another time might be more appropriate—" the marshal began, but Lydia cut him off.

"I know how you suffered seeing your dead wife's brooch. Forgive my forwardness, Marshal. The whole matter is so . . . upsetting." She rested her hand on the marshal's arm in a sympathetic gesture that seemed to isolate the two of them from the unpleasantness in the world.

"That it is, Miss Pressman, that it is. Go on and do what you need to do, if it makes you feel better." Gutherie motioned in the direction of Carstairs's bedroom. Lydia pushed past the lawman to find a half dozen large boxes on the floor around the bed. All of them were filled with rings, necklaces, brooches, and other jewelry. Lydia dived in and burrowed around.

"Women," grumbled Gutherie, watching Lydia methodically search the contents of the boxes. After Lydia had checked every carton twice, she sat back on her heels and looked stricken.

"Nothing," she said.

"He might have more stashed around," Gutherie said.

"Where? Let me look!"

"Settle down now, Miss Pressman. This is all we've found so far. All I meant was that Carstairs might have more that we haven't unearthed yet."

"You'll let me know if you find anything? Please, Marshal?"

"Of course," Gutherie said. As Fargo led a disconsolate Lydia from the room, Gutherie grabbed Fargo's arm and said to him, "You stay in town until the trial. I don't want this ghoul getting off scot-free."

"I've never seen so many people turn out for a trial," Lydia said, snuggling closer to Fargo in spite of how stifling the courthouse had become. More than a hundred men and women crowded in to witness justice being carried out.

"They ought to hang Carstairs and get on with the real trials," Fargo said. He was unhappy that Schatten walked the streets as a free man, out on bail after the marshal caught him near the dock along the Great Salt Lake shore. No trial date had been set for Lamont and the Utah Kid yet, either. Murder was not commonplace in Great Salt Lake City, but it happened often enough that it did not completely capture the public's imagination or indignation.

But an undertaker stealing from the dead was so extraordinary that it drew spectators from all around town. In one respect, Fargo could not blame the citizens. How many of them had been affected by Carstairs's thievery? From what he knew of most towns, the answer might be damned near all of them.

It struck him as odd the way Carstairs sat complacently. Not once had he shown any remorse or fear at what the court might mete out in the way of punishment. Fargo wondered if it came from putting on the false face of sincerity and mock shared grief, or if there was something dead in Carstairs's soul.

Whatever the cause of his calmness, it would be shaken soon enough. The judge came in and the trial began.

"There's no need to tell me what the charges are," the judge remarked, looking sour. "I've already gone over them."

"Then let the jury go deliberate and—" began the prosecutor.

"Shut up, Ben. There's not going to be a trial."

A silence fell over the courtroom, slowly replaced by furious whispering and eventually by the prosecutor's outraged demand for an explanation.

"Don't go callin' me names, Ben. You might be my cousin, but I'm keepin' order in this court," the judge said, glaring at the prosecutor. "I've looked over the charges, and if it were up to me, I'd trip the lever on the gallows for this miscreant." The judge glared at Carstairs, who sat quietly with his lawyer.

"But there's not going to be an execution because there's not going to be a trial."

"Why not?" asked the prosecutor, stunned.

"As despicable as what Carstairs has done, I can't find anything that says he broke any law in Utah."

"He stole my Sarah's necklace!" yelled someone in the back of the courtroom.

"As Carstairs's lawyer has pointed out, there's no law saying it's illegal to take property from a corpse. Who out on the trail hasn't found a canteen or a blanket its deceased owner couldn't use and took it for his own?"

"It's not the same!" protested the prosecutor. "He didn't need any of the jewelry to stay alive. Or the clothes, or—"

"Be quiet, Ben. The law doesn't cover taking things off a dead body. If he had dug 'em up, there might be a case

53

for grave robbing, but he took what he did 'fore they were put into the ground.''

Fargo shifted uneasily on the hard bench. From what the judge said, he was more likely a criminal than Carstairs because he had opened 'Rone's grave, although he had not removed anything. There hadn't been anything left to steal because Carstairs had already taken it.

"The dead can't own property and the living have given it up with no expectation of ever using it again. Carstairs committed no crime.''

"He stole from the dead!"

"Silence!" shouted the judge. "Bailiff, if there's another outburst from the spectators, I want the court emptied.''

The judge glowered at Carstairs, who smiled now.

"You are the lowest of the low, and by the criminal statutes I can't charge you with anything, since robbing a corpse not in the ground is not illegal. However, I am finding you guilty of contempt of court. As punishment, I order you exiled to Frémont Island out in the middle of the lake.''

"Wait, you can't do that! I'll pay a fine, but you can't exile me!'' The outburst was the first show of emotion from Carstairs.

"You're lucky I don't find other reasons for keeping you away from society. Marshal Gutherie, get some men together to escort him out to the island right away.''

"Judge, you want us to leave food with him?" spoke up the marshal.

The judge hesitated as he considered the situation, then nodded curtly.

"Wait, wait!" screamed Carstairs. "How long are you going to keep me out there like some animal?''

The judge's answer was muffled in the roar of approval that went up from the spectators. Exiling Carstairs seemed almost as popular as hanging him would have been.

"I reckon the laws are going to change after this," Fargo said, standing. On the frontier, justice was more immediate and perhaps crueler, but to Fargo it also seemed fairer. Carstairs deserved more than exile, but the law was the law. From the judge's look of disgust, Fargo knew he had given Carstairs the maximum sentence allowable.

It made Fargo hanker to move on. But first he had one

last obligation to fulfill. He had promised 'Rone as he lay dying he would help Lydia however he could.

Fargo pushed through the crowd and found the marshal dispatching two men to take Carstairs to Frémont Island.

"What can I do for you, Fargo?" The marshal was in no mood for small talk. Fargo did not blame him after finding out what Carstairs had done was not illegal.

"Miss Pressman wants to know if you've found anything more of 'Rone's."

"I've got a couple deputies searching the funeral parlor," the marshal said glumly. "They've turned up a few more boxes. I do declare, that man stole anything that went into a coffin with the corpse. The judge let him off too easy."

"I agree," said Lydia, crowding close, "but wouldn't it be fitting if all that Carstairs had stolen was returned to the families? I'd be glad to help in this fine pursuit."

Fargo knew this was Lydia's way of checking every item to be certain she did not miss anything of 'Rone's. He said nothing as the marshal mulled over the proposal.

"All right, Miss Pressman. I hadn't given it a lot of thought, how to deal with all that jewelry and clothing. It's going to leave Mrs. Carstairs buck naked, though. She didn't have any clothing Carstairs had not stolen."

Fargo shuddered at the notion of the undertaker's wife wearing only dead women's clothes. Mrs. Carstairs had to be as corrupt as her husband. Or did she even know where the clothing came from? She had not seemed to notice much of what went on around her, being the kind to accept whatever her husband told her.

"Show up at my office tomorrow morning, Miss Pressman, and we'll see about returning all that Carstairs has stolen." Gutherie nodded to Fargo, then left the courtroom.

Fargo felt the urge to move on, but he had to see that justice was done when Gus Lamont and the Utah Kid came to trial for 'Rone's murder. If Mormon law didn't convict them and Lester Schatten, then he would have to see to it himself.

Until then, he would help Lydia however he could, because he had promised his partner.

8

"Please, Skye, you're so important to me," pleaded Lydia Pressman. The brunette batted her long eyelashes and smiled winningly. Fargo felt his resolve melting as she moved closer, brushing tantalizingly against him.

"Marshal Gutherie is watching Schatten like a hawk, and there's nothing I can say at the trial that'll amount to a hill of beans. The marshal has Lamont's and the Utah Kid's confessions implicating Schatten. I feel useless now, and there's no reason for me to stay in town once the trial is over."

"Who cares about Schatten?" she said in exasperation, as if the man responsible for her fiancé's death no longer mattered. "I need company, to keep me from getting too lonely now that 'Rone is gone." She held him close. "You are such a comfort. I would miss you terribly if you left, and I think you'd miss me, too. Wouldn't you?"

"I'd think you would want to see Schatten with a rope around his neck for all he's done to you."

"Oh, Skye, of course I want to see justice done. It's just that when you're around, you remind me of 'Rone and all we had together. If you go, I won't have a thing left, of you or 'Rone. He thought the world of you, and so do I."

Fargo said nothing. Lydia had a few things to remind her of 'Rone, if that was what she wanted. The marshal had given her 'Rone's ring, although Fargo understood her squeamishness about it. The money was long gone, but Fargo had told Carstairs to keep it in way of payment for the burial. He should have insisted that the undertaker make good on returning even this paltry sum, but by now Carstairs was safely exiled to a desert island in the middle of the Great Salt Lake. No one was likely to visit him, except to take supplies to him, and Fargo wondered how long that would be done. Carstairs had lost any friends he might have had in town.

Surprising her with 'Rone's watch seemed the best way of pleasing her and fulfilling his promise to 'Rone, since that was about all the legacy his partner had left behind.

"We'll see," Fargo said, wondering what such a lovely woman saw in him when she could have her pick of any of the prosperous men in Great Salt Lake City. He knew he could pleasure her properly but did not kid himself that others in these parts weren't able to do likewise—and give Lydia a respectable future. Still, there was no accounting for taste. She had, after all, been ready to get hitched to 'Rone Clawson.

"Time's all I'm asking from you, Skye," she said, smiling at his acquiescence. "For now. Later, we'll see." A wicked gleam came into her eyes that told him more than her words ever could.

"I'd better escort you over to the marshal's office so you can see that everyone gets their due. I've got some scouting around to do on my own."

"It's my civic duty, and whatever business you have is likely to be similarly worthy." Again Lydia batted her long eyelashes, and Fargo knew he would likely stay on for a while after 'Rone's killers were sentenced.

She kissed him and then broke it off to smile brightly, reading him as if he were an open book. "You're a dear."

"First time anyone's ever called me that," Fargo said, not sure if he was being complimented or insulted for being so easily manipulated. He hitched the Ovaro to the back of Lydia's buggy, letting Lydia's horse pull the rig around to the front of the house where he helped her climb in. As before, she seemed lost in thought as they drove along. Fargo let her out at the marshal's office, then parked the buggy behind the jail.

He hesitated when he saw the window of the cell where Lamont and the Utah Kid were locked up. Waiting for them to be convicted was the main reason he stayed in Great Salt Lake City, them and the murderous Lester Schatten.

Stride long and determined, he walked down the alley to a main street. From there he went to Carstairs's funeral parlor, the front wall facing the street now spattered with rotten eggs and other viscous garbage. The windows had been broken out by rocks thrown by an unruly mob that Gutherie had done little to subdue earlier in the week. Fargo wondered if the marshal had not added a rock or two of his own to the melee.

He tried the front door, but it was secured on the inside, probably with a sturdy locking bar. Fargo went to the back and rattled the doorknob on the rear door. A bit of discreet pressure forced the door open. He slipped into the eerie interior of the mortuary.

Fargo felt like a grave robber in the deathly silent place.

The marshal and his deputies had combed the funeral parlor for any trinket the undertaker might have stolen, but Fargo repeated their route, carefully searching every room for any trace of 'Rone Clawson's missing watch. He emptied drawers filled with peculiar jagged-edged cutting devices and even looked behind bottles of pungent chemicals. Nowhere did he find a hidden cache of jewelry stolen from Carstairs's "clients."

Fargo looked around the room where Carstairs had worked on 'Rone's body. All the obvious places had been searched. He started testing the floor for loose boards, the walls for hidden safes, even the ceiling for a hollow where the undertaker might have hidden his ill-gotten gains. When Fargo finished with this room, he moved on to the other rooms, giving them a similar thorough going-over.

An hour later, he went into the viewing room and sank into a chair, staring morosely at the bier and the empty coffin on it. For all the trouble Carstairs had put everyone in Great Salt Lake City through, he ought to be in that coffin.

On impulse, Fargo got up and searched the coffin, thinking the mortician might have hidden something inside. There was no trace of any valuables stolen off the dead.

Disgusted at this waste of time, Fargo left the way he had entered. He had to reckon 'Rone's watch and anything else the man might have had on him was gone for good. Maybe a deputy had seen it while searching and had taken a fancy to it. Or one of the crowd might have pocketed it as he rampaged through the mortuary. The one thing Fargo knew for certain was that it had not been in the grave with 'Rone Clawson.

He walked slowly back to the marshal's office, figuring how best to tell Lydia she would have to be content with what of 'Rone's belongings she already had.

A line of silent men and women curled around the corner from the jail. Word of Lydia's mission to return what had been stolen must have spread like wildfire to get this many people out so fast. He pushed through the crowd and entered the marshal's office. Lydia sat in a chair at one side, the boxes of belongings at her feet. Fargo watched her for a minute, seeing how her intent gaze scrutinized every item she passed over after making a detailed notation of it in a book. No eagle had ever eyed its prey the way Lydia did, making sure the right person got the proper trinket.

An idea came to him as he watched her. There was one possibility he had overlooked. He went to her as she looked up.

"Can you get home by yourself?" he asked.

"Why, yes, of course, Skye," Lydia said. "I'm sure the marshal or one of his deputies would escort me, should the need arise."

"Good. I haven't quite finished my business yet." Fargo left the office before she could question him about his mission.

Carstairs knew what he did with everything he stole. He might be exiled on Frémont Island, but that didn't mean Fargo couldn't row out and talk to him. He might be willing to talk to the devil by now, especially if there was even a hint of someone putting in a good word for him with the judge.

Fargo wondered if he ought to ask Marshal Gutherie's permission or maybe go to the judge to see if Carstairs was allowed to have visitors. He imagined how the citizens of Great Salt Lake City would react if they discovered he had visited the disgraced undertaker. He stood at a dock and stared across the gently heaving surface of the lake toward the dots of desert islands in the middle, then came to a decision.

A slow grin crossed his lips. He might not have to expend the effort of talking to Carstairs at all. The one obvious victim in the entire sordid matter had been overlooked by everyone else. Fargo mounted his Ovaro and rode to the Carstairs house. His nose twitched as he approached. The house had received the same treatment as the funeral parlor in the middle of town.

"Mrs. Carstairs!" he called. "Can I talk to you for a minute? I don't mean you any harm." Fargo was not sure if the woman had remained in town, much less in the house. Somehow, though, he was not too surprised when the door opened slowly and the woman peered out timidly.

"Who are you?" She poked her head out a bit farther, then made a face as if she had bitten into something sour. "I know you! You're the one who had my husband arrested!"

Fargo was not going to debate the matter with her. He stopped at the foot of the steps leading to the steps leading to the small front porch.

"Ma'am, what he did was a terrible thing. I can see someone being tempted once or even twice, but your husband robbed the dead as a matter of business. That was wrong."

"I always loved the fine clothing he brought me. He is so very generous," the woman said, a small smile on her lips as she remembered better days.

"I'm looking for a watch. One in particular that belonged to my partner, 'Rone. Moroni Clawson was his full name, and he was one of the last men your husband buried.You ever see your husband with it?"

"He did have a new one. One with a fancy gold case. I'm not sure if he mentioned a Mr. Clawson, however."

Fargo glowered. He doubted Carstairs told the woman the names of any of the dead people he robbed before burial. Mrs. Carstairs did not seem too likely to remember, even if he had. She was a little slow, perhaps touched in the head, clearly not the type to question her surroundings.

"Can you describe the watch a little better, Mrs. Carstairs? It's important to 'Rone's fiancée that she recover it as a memento to remember him by."

Fargo decided it was mighty important to him, too. Finding the watch discharged his obligation to 'Rone. Heading for the peace of the high country in the Wasatch Mountains began to matter more and more to him, in spite of leaving behind Lydia and all she offered. "He usually did not bother with a timepiece, but he liked this one. He had it on him when all the . . . people came."

"At the trial," Fargo said anxiously. "Carstairs had it during the trial?"

"Why, yes."

"Does he still have it? On Frémont Island?"

"I don't know. He did not give it to me. That's all I know." The woman paused and looked forlorn. "Will he bring me more nice clothes, mister?"

"I don't think so, ma'am," Fargo said, seeing Mrs. Carstairs was unable to understand what her husband had done or how it affected her. "Do you have family to help you out?"

"I have a sister in Ogden."

"Contact her and see if you can go live with her."

"Why, I think I shall. Thank you for such a good suggestion."

Fargo watched the woman go back into the house, a mixture of emotions running through him. He felt pity for her and nothing but contempt for Carstairs. The man had treated the woman well—but at the expense of everyone else in the city.

Overriding all that was a sense of triumph. He had to go to Frémont Island, and when he found Carstairs, he could get the watch for Lydia, since there didn't seem to be anything else of 'Rone's of any value, sentimental or otherwise.

He returned to the dockside, welcoming the cool twilight cloaking the nearby buildings. A dozen rowboats were moored along a long dock. Fargo doubted anyone would miss a leaky boat for a couple of hours. He got his bearings, figured out which was Frémont Island, then got in the boat and started rowing.

Very soon, he would recover 'Rone's watch, even if he had to beat Carstairs to get it, and that would put things right with Lydia and fulfill his obligation to 'Rone. Fargo put his back into rowing, sending the boat skimming over the salty water.

9

As Fargo rowed, he grew increasingly uneasy. He preferred to have solid ground under his feet rather than the pitching, leaky boat and vast expanses of dark, ugly water. He longed for his sturdy Ovaro to get him from one place to another on dry land. Barring that, he would settle for being on foot with nothing but dirt or sand as far as the eye could see.

The boat rocked precariously from side to side, as if it knew he was no sailor and wanted to toss him into the salty water. With the sunset, the wind whipped over the lake and caused choppy waves to break against the prow of the boat.

Fargo rowed faster, his goal now in sight. Or at least he thought it was Frémont Island. He had taken the best fix on it he could while still on the dock and thought he kept it lined up with the front of the rowboat. Occasional glances over his shoulder warned him of other small islands dotting the Great Salt Lake.

For all he knew, the two men who had been responsible for getting Carstairs out here had chosen some other island. Frémont Island was no different from the others, as far as he could tell. Worse, he had too much time to think about this fool's errand he was on.

He had taken it into his head that Lydia ought to have 'Rone's watch because Carstairs had worn the ring. Why wouldn't she think the watch was equally tainted because the undertaken had shoved it into his vest pocket? Fargo had promised 'Rone he would look after Lydia, not go on wild-goose chases for a watch that probably wouldn't fetch ten dollars unless the buyer was feeling downright charitable.

Fargo considered going to a jewelry store and buying a

watch to give to Lydia. The lie wouldn't be too bad if he told her this was her beloved's timepiece—but it would still be a lie and one she might uncover right away. Fargo had no way of knowing how good a look Lydia had gotten of 'Rone's timepiece. Most of all, lying went against Fargo's grain, even when the fib was intended to ease a grieving woman's mind.

The boat rocked even more as the wind picked up. He started getting a little queasy with the lift and drop of the boat, and rowing became more difficult as the waves rose a foot or two in front of the rowboat.

When Lamont, the Utah Kid and Schatten went to trial and were convicted, he would move on. Fargo doubted that could come soon enough to suit him. He wanted nothing more than for Great Salt Lake City, a dead partner, and the ghoulish memory of Carstairs's crime to be behind him—far behind him. The only regret he would have was Lydia Pressman. She was a fine woman.

The boat hit a rock and jolted Fargo enough that he almost toppled overboard. He recovered and used his left oar to push away from the rock. Then it came to him. He had to be close to an island or he wouldn't have banged into a submerged rock. He twisted about and saw he had almost beached the rowboat on one of the desert islands.

He hoped it was Frémont Island and that he could find Carstairs quickly to find out about the watch. Fargo used the oar to push against the sloping sandy lake bottom and get ashore. He jumped out, grabbed the frayed rope on the prow and dragged the boat onto the gravelly beach. Having the boat drift back onto the choppy lake was the last thing he wanted. It was a mighty long swim to shore, even if the salt water made floating easier.

Fargo touched the Colt at his hip, then started his hunt for the undertaker. A slice of moon rose high enough to let him see the ground clearly. Five minutes brought him to a spot where another boat had beached recently. The tracks leading from it were too windblown to read easily, but he reckoned they had to belong to Carstairs and the two men who had brought him to the island.

Following the tracks inland led him to a small stand of scrubby trees stunted by the salt water and on to a small lean-to.

"Carstairs! I want to talk to you. Where are you hiding, you miserable son of a bitch?" Fargo sucked in his breath when he realized this was not likely to be the way to get the undertaker to show himself. Carstairs might think Fargo had come to kill him.

"I don't want to hurt you. I want to dicker. I'll see what I can do to get you off the island in exchange for something you stole off my partner."

Fargo cocked his head to one side and listened hard. Few men knew how to listen better than the Trailsman, and he heard nothing but the wind blowing through the vegetation and the waves from the Great Salt Lake lapping on the shores of Frémont Island.

"Carstairs?"

Fargo's heart began to pound harder. The undertaker had been cool and collected in the court until the judge had sentenced him. A man that reserved having his world turned upside down might become desperate. He might even think on killing himself.

In a way, that made Fargo's mission easier. It would be a fitting irony if all he had to do was take the watch off Carstairs's worthless corpse.

"Carstairs, where are you?" As Fargo began exploring the island, it came to him that the undertaker would have a hard time committing suicide. There weren't any trees with sturdy enough limbs to hang oneself. The men who had brought him to the island on the judge's orders would not have been foolish enough to leave a knife or other weapon with him. It was not difficult to sharpen a short stick and use it to stab, but Fargo had a hard time thinking Carstairs would be that desperate.

Yet.

He studied the ground around the lean-to and saw that Carstairs had indeed spent some time here. But if the two men who had exiled him had also left supplies, Fargo could not find them. He began circling the camp and found a solitary set of prints leading to the far side of the island. There was a curious furrow behind the tracks that partially erased them, but this made tracking easier. Thinking Carstairs might have gone hunting—exactly for what on this barren patch of sandy nothing Fargo was at a loss to figure—he got on the trail and followed it to the side of the island away from view of anyone in the city.

"I'll be damned," Fargo said when he figured out what had happened. From the debris on the shoreline, a boat had wrecked here. It appeared as if Carstairs, always followed by the deep furrow in the dirt, had spent some time working in the area. Fargo guessed the undertaker had repaired the beached boat and must have taken off for the far shore.

"So much for exiling the son of a bitch," he grumbled. Fargo made a circuit of the small island to be sure Carstairs was not hiding, then returned to his own rowboat and the difficult trip back to the docks.

Fargo cursed himself all the way for being such a fool.

Fargo patted the Ovaro and gentled the spirited horse. He rubbed his hands against his buckskins, trying to make his palms stop stinging. He had thought he had calluses from good, honest work to harden his hands, but rowing had shown him a different kind of chore. The salt water stung his eyes, and the rough board seat in the rowboat had put splinters into his behind.

In spite of all that and learning of Carstairs's escape, Fargo was in a genial mood. He had the feeling that he would track down the undertaker in a hurry now that he knew the man had rowed to the far side of the lake. This was his territory, and no one was a better tracker. Carstairs didn't have a ghost of a chance of getting away from him once he was on the trail.

Riding slowly, Fargo followed a well-traveled narrow trail around the lake. The wind whistled noisily and the waves crashed against rocks, sending salt spray high into the air and drenching him. He ignored the discomfort and kept a steady pace until a little after midnight, when he found a stand of sheltering junipers and dozed.

At first light, the Trailsman again hunted for Carstairs. He lost sight of Frémont Island now and then as the shoreline curved away from the desert island, but his innate sense of direction kept him moving. Carstairs could have come to shore miles away, but on foot he would not get far.

The other side of the world was not far enough to run. When Fargo found a decrepit rowboat pulled up on shore about where he thought Carstairs would have landed, he knew the hunt was nearing an end.

He jumped to the ground and looked over the boat. How Carstairs had gotten it this far was a mystery. Holes bigger than a .44 slug peppered the bottom. Carstairs would have had to row and bail constantly to reach the shore in this leaky craft. Dropping to one knee, Fargo saw the curious trail he had noticed on Frémont Island. Light footprints were obscured by a heavier furrow that partially obliterated them.

If Carstairs was trying to hide his tracks, he was doing a terrible job of it.

Fargo followed the footprints and the deep rut along the shore, then angled up toward the road circling the lake. He stopped and stared when he found what had caused the furrow—he saw a ball and chain lying on the dirt path. Carstairs had used a rock to break open the shackle holding him to the heavy iron ball. This was the way they had intended to keep him on Frémont Island. Otherwise, he could have swum away, if he dared—or boredom drove him to it.

Knowing the man had the ball and chain on during the trip from the island, rowing and bailing, in the dark across a choppy lake, warned him of how desperate Carstairs was to escape.

He mounted his Ovaro and rode slowly, keeping the undertaker's footprints in sight. Carstairs headed north into the mountains, terrain Fargo knew better than the back of his own hand. He picked up the pace after midafternoon, wanting to overtake the escaping undertaker before sunset.

The scent of pines and the fresh wind devoid of any hint of salt invigorated Fargo. He was following a city dweller who made no effort to hide his tracks. The summer Utah day was beautiful, and he felt confident he would overtake Carstairs soon. Everything was perfect until the rock struck him on the side of the head, knocking him from his saddle. Flailing, Fargo fell heavily and landed with a crash amid a carpet of pine needles. Momentarily stunned, he lay still as he tried to get his wits about him again.

The faint *slip-slip-slip* of someone approaching warned him he was not tangling with the undertaker. Whoever came for him moved like the wind, soft, silent, and deadly.

When he judged the time right, Fargo rolled fast and dragged out his six-shooter.

He thumbed back the Colt and fired at the Indian rushing up, knife held high to kill him. The bullet raked across the brave's chest, leaving a crease that was bloodier than it was dangerous. Before Fargo could fire a second time, the warrior was on him. The knife drove straight for his throat, forcing him to drop his six-gun to grab a brawny wrist and wrestle it to one side.

The brave lost his balance and fell away. Fargo followed, getting his legs wrapped around the warrior's middle. Squeezing with his powerful legs and pummeling the Indian, Fargo fought for his life. He felt a flash of pain as the brave dragged the sharp knife along his ribs, then it was all over in a heartbeat.

The Indian drew blood, but Fargo got both his hands around the man's wrist. Twisting hard, he turned the point around and then used his weight to drive the brave's own knife into his gut. The Indian twitched once, then died.

Fargo pushed back from the dead man, gasping for air. He had almost died and had no idea why. He rubbed the goose-egg lump growing on the side of his head, then reached down and jerked free from the Indian's belt a slingshot with two long leather straps and an attached pocket made from deer hide and decorated with bird feathers. From the pattern, Fargo could see his ambusher had been a Crow warrior.

The Indian had been out hunting for small game and had attacked Fargo instead. The run-in he had had with other Crows while scouting for Captain Simpson ought to have alerted him that they had been riled again and were out protecting their territory.

He stood and looked around, worrying that the Crow had not been alone. The attack had been sudden but not planned. No Crow came after a frontiersman with only a slingshot and knife. If the Indian had been on the warpath, he could have been carrying a rifle or a bow and arrow. Fargo realized how fortunate he had been.

Fargo searched the Indian, but found nothing of interest. A hunter out for rabbit or birds. But his lack of other equipment told Fargo a Crow encampment was somewhere nearby. He chewed his lower lip, considering what to do.

He was on Carstairs's trail and had to be close enough to overtake him in a few minutes. Finding him to return him to his exile seemed a more important chore now than recovering 'Rone's watch. Justice had to be served, and Carstairs could not be allowed to escape.

But the Indians posed a special problem.

Fargo had no quarrel with them. If they wanted the army and the settlers out of the area, that was not his fight. But he doubted any Crow war chief was likely to sit down to palaver before shooting first.

"Come on," Fargo said, tugging at the horse's reins. The Ovaro whinnied and followed him as he sought Carstairs's footprints again. The rockier ground made tracking more difficult, but the undertaker had not tried to hide his trail. Fargo's long strides devoured the ground until he came to a game path.

Here he had to decide which direction Carstairs had taken, left or right. The dirt on the narrow trail was packed down hard, and more than one deer had come along to cut up the ground and obscure the trail. Fargo sniffed the air and caught the scent of water about the same time his horse did.

He decided to head uphill. Carstairs had wanted to get away from town. Up the slope and deeper into the mountains seemed the most likely way for the fleeing undertaker to have headed.

It was also where the Crow hunting party was most likely to lie in wait for game.

Fargo found that out the hard way when an arrow suddenly winged past him and buried itself inches deep into a tree trunk beside the path. He spun, ready to hightail it back down the path, only to see dark shadows moving from the trees and onto the trail to block his way.

He was caught between two bands of Crow hunters, both of them willing to lift his scalp.

10

Fargo froze and stared at the Crows silhouetted by pale moonlight on the game trail. He had passed a pair of hunters and had never noticed them in their hiding places. Or more likely they had come up after he had gone by. It didn't matter. Fargo was caught between Indians ahead and behind.

He dropped and rolled to one side, narrowly avoiding another arrow fired by the Crow hunter on his right. The Crows weren't using rifles, which led him to believe that they were either a poor band or that they had reason to avoid making loud noises. This convinced Fargo he had a chance to get away. They weren't on the warpath hunting for scalps, not caring how much ruckus they raised. They sought a few deer or maybe a bear to take back to their tribe.

That did not mean he was going to get away without showing some mighty fine survival skills. After all, they had fired on him without so much as asking him who he was. That meant they were as inclined to rob a careless traveler as they were to bag a buck. Fargo rolled and, coming to his feet, he swung around a rough-barked ponderosa pine tree, pressed his back into it, waited a heartbeat, then whirled about, swinging the butt of his Colt at shoulder level. He had not seen the brave hot on his trail but had sensed his attack. Catching the Indian across the throat, Fargo took out the brave, who collapsed with a choking sound.

Fargo went back into a crouch, paused beside the still-convulsing body, then exploded upward. He tackled the next brave as he approached and bore him to the ground, arms hanging on to the scissoring legs as the Indian kicked to get free. The Crow was taken by surprise, and this allowed Fargo to swarm on top of him. Again Fargo's Colt rose and fell, slugging the man alongside the head. The first blow did not knock out the Crow, but the second did.

He wasted no time to see if the other hunters were coming after him. Staying off the trail but running parallel to it in the darkness, Fargo retreated. The sound of breaking twigs and crushed vegetation left a track a blind man could follow, but Fargo feared other Indians lying in wait along the trail. He might have given them an easy trail to follow, but he had also avoided an ambush.

When he had gone a hundred yards through the undergrowth, he cut perpendicular to the path and plunged into the less densely overgrown wooded area. The fir and blue spruce here were scrubby and afforded little protection, so Fargo knew he had to keep running—fast.

He had not gone far when he was forced to slow because of increasingly dense undergrowth barring his way. Fargo again changed direction and ran a few more yards, trying not to leave much trail now. When he had gone far enough, he went into the lowest limbs of a pine tree, jumping, grabbing hold, and pulling himself up. Lying belly down on a branch seven feet off the ground, he waited for the pursuit he knew would come. Less than five minutes passed before he heard a faint sound like a branch brushing against buckskins. Fargo tensed. Beneath him crept a Crow hunter, moving rapidly but still alert.

The Indian stopped, sniffed the air, and looked around. Fargo aimed his six-shooter at the Crow, should the Indian find his hiding place. The Crow turned in a full circle, then went back to stalking his prey. Fargo watched the Indian vanish into the darkness.

On the heels of the first brave came a second and a third. Each time a Crow passed, Fargo was certain he would be discovered. But not one looked up into the limbs to see their quarry.

After the third hunter went into the forest, Fargo waited almost a half hour before dropping to the ground. He landed lightly and stayed low, making sure he was alone. The Crows had given up chasing him, but a dilemma faced him that had not existed before.

Should he keep after Carstairs in spite of the Crows

being out for blood, or should he leave the man to his fate? Fargo had avoided the Indians, but Carstairs was no woodsman and would fall easy prey to the hunting party.

A streak of stubbornness caused Fargo to make his way back to the game trail where he had been attacked. Carstairs had been lucky, passing through before the Crow hunting party had settled in to wait for game.

Or had he been so lucky?

Fargo knew the Indians fairly well, having scouted with them and against them for the army. They were patient hunters, willing to spend an entire night in one place if they thought the game would come by eventually. An unwary tenderfoot like Carstairs might have become a victim.

The game trail had been cut up by at least one deer's hooves since the Crows had chased Fargo away. He lay flat on his stomach and sighted along the ground for any other sign. It took Fargo more than twenty minutes to find what had to be Carstairs's footprint. When he did, Fargo let out a low sigh. From the way the grass was trampled down around the footprint in the softer dirt beside the trail, Fargo knew the Indians had caught the undertaker.

Fargo knew he had to be sure Carstairs was not going to be killed by the Indians, as much as the undertaker deserved such a hideous end. The judge had sentenced Carstairs to exile, not death, and Fargo intended to see that the undertaker was properly punished according to the law.

His every sense alert, Fargo pressed on, traveling more than an hour before catching the sharp scent of burning pine. The Indian camp was nearby. He crept forward and saw a bigger hunting party than he had anticipated. More than a dozen braves sat around small fires, warming their hands and talking low amongst themselves. Even more huddled by the fires underneath blankets, asleep.

Fargo knew he had to work fast. Dawn lay only an hour off. If he did not find Carstairs and rescue him by then, the Crows were likely to move their camp. Either Carstairs would be taken along as a prisoner, or he would be killed. Fargo didn't have a ghost of a chance of saving the undertaker by fighting so many hunters.

The Crows had not posted sentries around their hunting camp, making his surveillance easier. Fargo circled the camp and finally spotted Carstairs away from most of the fires. He swallowed hard when he saw how the Indians had bound the undertaker's legs with a hobble and then tied a rawhide thong around his neck. The long leather strap snaked off into the dark, undoubtedly secured to a stake to keep Carstairs from escaping.

Worse, they had stripped off Carstairs's clothing and crudely dressed him as a squaw. If they allowed Carstairs to live and took him back to the rest of the tribe, he would be treated as the lowest of the low, forced to do menial chores even the Crow women refused to do. He would be spit upon and ridiculed and forced to live a marginal existence on garbage. His life on Frémont Island had been dismal. As a Crow slave, it would be far worse, with daily abuse and backbreaking work.

Fargo reached down and slid his Arkansas toothpick from a boot sheath, then wiggled forward on his belly until he was a few feet from the undertaker. Carstairs looked up from where he sat disconsolately, startled when Fargo hissed to get his attention.

"I'm here to free you," Fargo said, grabbing the thong and placing the knife blade against it.

"Thank Heaven!" cried Carstairs, so loudly that Fargo jumped. "They are monsters!"

"Quiet, you fool!"

But the damage had been done. Two sleeping braves jerked up, looking around. They shuffled off their blankets and drew knives, intent on finding what caused Carstairs's outburst.

Fargo knew better than to tackle both men with an entire camp able to come to their assistance should it be needed. He sheathed his Arkansas toothpick and got to his feet, running like all the demons of hell were on his trail.

And as far as Fargo was concerned, they were.

The two Indians let out loud whoops and came after him. He reached a wooded area by the time the first brave caught up. A powerful hand shot out, shoving Fargo off balance. He fell forward, somersaulted, and came to his feet still running. His foe was also off balance, but the second Crow following him was not. With another loud yell, the Indian pounced on Fargo.

Knowing he dared not stay to fight, Fargo threw the Crow over his shoulder and kicked out. His boot crashed into the Indian's kneecap, buckling his leg. Taking the opportunity, Fargo disappeared into the woods, using every bit of his skill to avoid the second Crow coming after him.

He circled, he dodged, he did all he could to hide his trail. And it worked. Just before dawn turned the sky pearly with the light of a new day, Fargo knew he had lost the Indians pursuing him.

He hunkered down, hiding in a clump of bushes to think. Carstairs was a prisoner, a slave. Fargo owed the undertaker nothing but did not like to think of what dire fate lay ahead of him.

Fargo knew that the Crow camp would be awake and preparing to leave. They were hunters and, depending on their success, would want to return soon to their summer encampment with their game. Rescuing Carstairs by sneaking in and spiriting him away from underneath the Crows' noses was no longer possible, even for the Trailsman.

If he wanted to return Carstairs to Great Salt Lake City and his court decreed sentence, he had to adopt a more direct approach.

After he checked his Colt, Fargo slid the knife from his boot and made sure it was nice and sharp. Then he stood, took a deep breath, and did what had to be done. He marched straight into the Crow camp.

The boldness of his entry took the Indians by surprise. They stood silently, watching as he walked to the center of the camp.

"I welcome my brothers, the fearless Crow, to my land. Your hunt has gone well. That is testimony to your great skill."

"Who are you?" A Crow equaling Fargo in height but outweighing him by twenty pounds came through the ring of watching Indians. This had to be the chief of the hunting party. Fargo sized him up fast. Heavier—stronger. The Crow chief might even be faster.

"Do the Crow forget their manners while hunting in my land?" asked Fargo.

"This is not your land. It is *ours*!" the chief protested. Fargo kept from smiling. He had distracted them from lifting his scalp to argue over on whose land they hunted. Fargo had no idea who owned this land, if anyone. It might well be Crow territory.

"I am a gracious host. You may hunt as you please on my land," Fargo said, oblivious to the chief's protest. He waved his arm around to encompass the entire Crow camp. "All of you are welcome."

"Who are you?" demanded the chief.

Fargo was glad that the two braves who had chased him were nowhere to be seen. They might have recognized him, or at least thought it suspicious that one white man had tried to free their prisoner only an hour before another waltzed into their camp.

"I am called the Trailsman."

The Crow spoke among themselves, some nudging others and lifting chins to point out Fargo to others farther back in the crowd. His reputation was known throughout the West, even among the Indians.

"You are our enemy, white man," the chief said, thrusting out his chest. His chin jutted at a belligerent angle, and his stance spoke of arrogance. Fargo could not let this go unchallenged. And he did not want to. This was what he had hoped for.

"I am not your enemy," Fargo said, speaking loudly. "You are mine. You come onto my land to hunt. I permit this. But you have also taken my brother prisoner. Free him. Let my brother go."

The words tasted like acid on his tongue. A cow pie like Carstairs was not his brother in any way. If he had been the judge, Fargo would have had Carstairs hanged on the spot rather than exiling him for what he had done. But Fargo was not going to allow anyone to be a slave to the Crow tribe. Even Carstairs deserved a better end than that.

"He insulted me. He is my squaw man," the chief said, sneering.

"Does it take so little to insult you?" asked Fargo, hoping to anger the chief further. "He is nothing and yet you allow this nothing to insult you? What kind of chief are you? A chief of an insignificant people?"

The Crow roared with rage and grabbed for Fargo. Fargo was ready. He spun to one side, letting the Indian fall past. A leg shot out and tangled up the chief's feet, bringing him down onto his face. Fargo hopped around and put his foot squarely in the middle of the chief's back, holding him for a moment.

"Yes, I see it clearly now. You are a chief of no skill."

This caused a murmur to rise in the hunting party. Fargo walked a narrow line now. If he pushed too hard, he would be peppered with arrows, but if he failed to acquit himself honorably now, and show he was as brave as any in the camp, he was a goner, too.

He took his foot off the chief and stepped back.

"You cannot anger me this way. I still permit you to hunt on my land. Give me back my white brother."

"No!"

The chief jumped to his feet. His hands balled into tight fists, ready to explode at any instant. Fargo worked to keep the chief's anger in check.

"Will you show your strength in a duel for Carstairs, for my white brother?" Fargo asked.

"A duel?"

"I challenge you to leg wrestling. The winner chooses my white brother's fate." Fargo was a powerful man, but he gambled with Carstairs's life as well as his own.

"You win, you take the white squaw man? And if I win?" The Crow chief turned cagey. "Do I also have the famous Trailsman as a squaw?" A laugh went up throughout the assembled Crows.

"You won't win." Fargo stated it quietly, simply. This caused a hush to fall over the boisterous hunters.

"Here. Now." The chief pointed to a level spot in the camp. He strutted over, then turned to face Fargo.

Fargo walked up and faced the chief. They locked their left arms together, then sank to the ground on their backs. Fargo's head was to the north and the Crow's to the south.

"Whenever you're ready," Fargo challenged.

The chief lifted his left leg high in the air. Fargo rolled back a little on his shoulders and locked his left knee around the Crow's. The contest of strength began. Fargo crunched down hard, his belly screaming in pain as the muscles tightened like steel bands. Using his leg, Fargo fought to drive the chief's leg back toward his opponent's chest. Fargo coordinated his efforts, adding the effects of his arm and shoulder and belly to that of the powerful muscles in his leg, playing on weakness he felt in the Crow's attack.

For a few seconds, the fight was in doubt. Then Fargo's

superior tactics won the day. Inch by inch, his leg forced back the Indian's. The chief doubled over and then somersaulted backward, defeated.

Fargo disengaged his arm and got to his feet. He had won.

11

"Bring me your prisoner," Fargo said loudly. "He's mine now!"

The Crow chief glared at him, his eyes smoldering with anger at the defeat. Fargo saw two men in the hunting party hurry off to obey him, which further infuriated the chief. It made it seem as if the interloping white eyes was in charge.

"You rescued me," cried Carstairs, tears streaming down his cheeks. "Thank you!" He took no notice how the Crows shoved him to the ground, then spat on him and tried to kick him. Carstairs's joy at being freed was so great he ignored everything around him, and that spelled danger for them both.

"Pull yourself together," Fargo snapped. To show any weakness in front of this many Crow warriors was a big mistake. They respected strength. This might have been why they decided to turn Carstairs into a slave for squaw work. He must have begged and pleaded for them to spare his life when they found him out in the forest.

The braves stirred restlessly, giving Fargo the feeling that the situation was like a pot on the verge of boiling over. He wanted to get away as fast as possible.

Then he remembered why he had pursued Carstairs this far.

"Where are your clothes?" Fargo said urgently. "And all your other belongings?"

"Th—they stripped me and gave me these rags," Carstairs stammered. The undertaker stared down at the squaw's clothing they had put on him, as if trying to figure out how this had come about. Fargo saw the man was in shock and wasn't likely to be much help.

Fargo walked to the chief and stared him in the eye. "Return all his clothing," he ordered. "Return anything else you stole from him." As it was, Fargo saw that he had gone too far with his bold approach ordering the humiliated chief about as he had.

The chief yanked out his knife and roared like a wild beast as he jumped Fargo. The sudden attack caught Fargo unawares. He barely threw up his left arm in time to keep the plunging knife from sinking into his chest. Sharp pain lanced up the length of his left forearm, but Fargo willed it away. He dropped to one knee and deflected what he could of the chief's dishonorable attack. As he turned to his left, Fargo drew his Arkansas toothpick with his right hand. The sharp tip rose and sank hilt deep into the Crow's belly.

A hot gush of blood told the end of the chief's life.

Fargo shoved hard and knocked the chief to the ground, where he kicked feebly, his dark eyes fixed in hatred on Fargo. He mumbled something, then died.

A deathly silence descended on the band of hunters. Fargo backed off, knowing the shock of seeing their chief die so swiftly would wear off soon. He was not sure what they would do then. The chief had violated tribal custom with his attack, but counting on the others in the hunting party to recognize that was not something Fargo wanted to bet his scalp on.

"Get out of here," he said to Carstairs. "Run. Do it now!"

Fargo backed from the chief's body, the gory knife clutched in his hand. Two warriors came up and knelt to examine the body of their slain leader. Then they both stood and let out war whoops that curdled Fargo's blood as they attacked.

Fargo lunged at the leading brave. Changing his style of attack, Fargo slashed at eye level. This forced the warrior back into the others following him into the fray. They went down in a tangle of arms and legs, struggling to get at their enemy and failing. Fargo saw he had a decision to make, and it had to be made fast. Carstairs had been circled by a half dozen braves and wasn't going to get away without help. If Fargo tried to save the undertaker, he was sure he would die trying. If he ran, he might escape intact.

Maybe.

Fargo ran for his life, thinking hard how to turn this to his advantage and save Carstairs. If he had stayed, he would have died in the overwhelming attack. By chasing him, the Indians divided their party and gave Fargo another chance at freeing the undertaker. He dodged through the woods, doubled back, circled, used every bit of his woodcraft skills to confuse and hide his tracks.

Every time he got within a few yards of the camp and Carstairs, however, he was forced back into the woods. He had survived, but the Crows thwarted him repeatedly because they thought he would return for Carstairs. After hours of relentless pursuit, the Crows finally gave up and returned to their camp—and their prisoner.

Exasperated at his failure to keep the Indian party divided, Fargo settled down and tended to the cut on his left arm. It had bled profusely from the chief's blade, but pressure on it had kept it from leaving a trail as Fargo ran. Now he had to tend to it or he would have a numbed, useless arm. He awkwardly bandaged the wound the best he could, then checked for any other wounds.

He had found the heat of battle often hid injuries that could betray him later. Fargo was pleased to find his hide was intact, save for the cut made by the dying Crow chief. He settled into a protected spot where he could think through his dilemma.

Carstairs had been easily recaptured and was once again in Crow captivity. Fargo took his inability to free the undertaker as a personal affront now, a challenge to his honor and abilities. After the morning's fight and the bloodshed, the Crows were likely to take their revenge on the mortician. All Fargo had to fight with were his Arkansas toothpick and a Colt.

And his wits.

He considered the matter more carefully. Bulling in had not worked any better than sneaking in to rescue Carstairs. He had run out of alternatives—or had he?

An idea came to him. It was a desperate plan that formed in his head, but Carstairs's life hung in the balance. He heaved himself to his feet and went back to the Crow campsite, wary of a trap. Fargo need not have worried. The Indians were preparing their chief's body for burial according to tribal custom. He spied on how they prepared the funeral pyre, then circled to find what they had done with Carstairs.

Fargo expected to find the undertaker dangling from a tree with his guts ripped out. Or perhaps, like the Apaches, they might cut off Carstairs's eyelids and force him to stare into the sun until he went blind and crazy. To Fargo's relief, they had done very little in the way of torturing their prisoner.

Stripped naked and staked out spread eagle, Carstairs moaned softly as he feebly tugged at the rawhide straps cruelly binding his ankles and wrists. Otherwise, they had done nothing to him.

Fargo watched carefully and soon discovered the reason for this lack of revenge-taking. Three Crow warriors had camouflaged themselves and were waiting patiently for him to come to the rescue. He knew that a tribe of the Crow's reputation would not have given up their pursuit so easily. They realized he had run, not out of fear for his own life, but to divide them to make rescuing Carstairs easier. Fargo slipped back into the deep woods, not willing to play their game.

He had another idea that just might work.

Fargo gathered dried leaves and broken limbs from trees, piling them against a dead log. From here he spent another half hour putting whatever flammable forest debris he could find in a low mound almost twenty yards long. He was as swift as he was quiet, although the Crows were plenty distracted with their burial ritual. He estimated the wind speed blowing at his back, how the fire would sweep through the Crow camp toward a swift stream nearby and be stopped from spreading too far, then hunkered down and began striking a piece of flint from the ground against the steel blade of his Arkansas toothpick.

Fat blue sparks jumped from the steel into the tinder-dry leaves. The sudden roar as the wood and leaves burst into flames knocked Fargo off his feet. He reached over and grabbed a burning branch and tossed it as hard as he could. He repeated this in the other direction and quickly had a ten-foot wall of flame blowing toward the Crows' camp.

Fargo wasted no time getting around the end of the blistering sheet of fire he had created, going directly to where Carstairs was staked out in the hot afternoon sun.

The forest fire flushed four Crow braves from hiding. Fargo was glad he had not rushed in earlier. He had spotted only three. The naked undertaker struggled and screamed as the Indians rushed off to their camp, abandoning him. Fargo knew he would never have a better chance to free the man.

"Keep your mouth shut," Fargo said, towering over the bound man. "Say one word and I'll cut your tongue out before I cut your bonds."

Carstairs's mouth opened, then snapped shut when he realized Fargo was not joking. Four quick *snicks* of the Arkansas toothpick parted the rawhide strips binding Carstairs to the stakes. The man got to his feet and took a few unsteady steps. He used an arm to shield his face against the intense heat from the fire.

"I didn't have much choice," Fargo explained. He didn't like setting the fire, but it forged a deadly wall between him and the Crows. The Indians would be forced to cross the stream, giving Fargo added time to escape.

"We'll burn up!" Carstairs cried. Fargo glared at him, and the undertaker subsided, only gasping as he strained to keep up the swift pace Fargo set.

"We won't. The fire will burn itself out in a few minutes unless the wind shifts." Fargo kept Carstairs moving, alert to the direction of the wind. It continued to blow against his face, meaning that the fire would reach the stream and be quenched any time now.

Wary of pursuit by the Indians, Fargo hesitated when they reached the edge of the forest away from the fire. He had lost track of why he had sought out Carstairs in the first place. Carstairs was buck naked and any chance of retrieving 'Rone's watch was now long gone, since the fire ravaged the Crow camp. Over the dying crackle of the flames, Fargo heard the fleeing Indians. They were in complete disarray, scattered over half the mountainside.

With their chief dead and a new one not yet elected, no one was likely to rally them against Fargo and come after an escaped slave.

"Come on," Fargo said, knowing there was no point in searching the camp for Carstairs's belongings. The clothes and more importantly 'Rone's watch were both destroyed by now.

"Can I thank you?" Carstairs asked timidly. "You said you'd cut my tongue out, but I want to thank you for—"

"Shut up," Fargo said. He lengthened his stride, forcing Carstairs to hurry after him. The undertaker moaned and sobbed to himself as his feet were cut repeatedly by sharp stones along the game path.

"Please, can we stop? Just for a minute?" Carstairs was sobbing openly now. Fargo hated the undertaker as much for his weakness as he did himself for giving in.

"Only for a minute," he said, slipping off the trail and indicating Carstairs should do the same. Fargo chose to walk through a blackberry bramble that tore at Carstairs's naked flesh.

"Why are you doing this to me?" Carstairs asked.

"You don't feel any remorse at all for stealing off dead people, do you?"

"Why should I? They had no need for their trinkets."

Fargo clenched his fists, then relaxed a mite. This was a man whose mind was totally alien to him, a man without morals in a city built on religious ideals. It made no sense, possibly because the contrast between the Mormon faith and such dastardly thievery was so great.

"What happened to the watch?" Fargo asked, wanting to put the matter to rest once and for all. He had pried Carstairs loose from his captors, and getting him back to Frémont Island or whatever new punishment the judge might hand down was only a matter of time. Fargo wanted to satisfy his promise to 'Rone and surprise Lydia with a memento to remind her of her betrothed—and Skye Fargo.

"Watch?"

"The one you had at the trial. Your wife said you took it off 'Rone Clawson's body and kept it for yourself."

"I did do that."

"So? Where is it?"

"You want that watch, don't you? What's it worth to you?" Carstairs turned sly.

"Your miserable hide," Fargo said coldly. "I rescued you because I didn't want you escaping your lawful sentence. There's no reason for me to risk my neck like I did, otherwise."

"So it *is* important." Carstairs gloated as he rubbed his hands together like a banker contemplating a foreclosure. "You need me to recover it."

"I don't need you for anything," Fargo said. "The watch is gone, lost back in the fire. If the Crows didn't steal it, then it was still with your clothing and got burned up."

"You think so?"

Fargo hesitated. The man showed remarkable presence for being as naked as a jaybird. He had recovered his wits well after the fright of being the Crows' prisoner. It was as if he had found a well-rehearsed role and knew how to play it.

"I'm taking you back to Great Salt Lake City and the marshal. He can figure what to do with you since you got off Frémont Island so easily. Might be this time, they'll stretch your neck."

"I did nothing illegal," Carstairs said haughtily. Then in an arrogant tone he added, "I know where the watch is. I'm willing to barter for it."

"Your freedom for the watch? I don't think so," Fargo said. He started to order Carstairs back to the game trail leading toward the lakeshore when he heard stealthy movement in the forest behind him. Fargo slipped his Arkansas toothpick from its boot sheath. The movement caused Carstairs to get the wrong idea.

"Don't kill me!" he cried. "I *do* know where the watch is—and it's not in the Indian camp!"

"Run," Fargo ordered. "Get on the trail and run for your life."

Carstairs thought Fargo meant to kill him. He lit out, his bare feet pounding on the hard-packed earth. As he bolted like a frightened fawn, Fargo crouched and began to duck-walk. The brambles he had pushed Carstairs through now served as a shield between him and the Crow hunter stalking through the forest.

Fargo wondered if this nightmare of killing would ever end. He saw the brave pass by, arrow nocked and ready to shoot. When the sound of Carstairs's mad flight for safety reached the Crow's ears, he vaulted over the blackberry brambles and hit the trail to take off after the fleeing undertaker.

This gave Fargo the chance he needed. He came up behind the Indian, slashing his knife furiously. There had been too much killing already. Fargo's intent was not to slice off the Crow's head but to sever the man's bowstring. When the toothpick's steel edge dragged over the bowstring, the taut gut string parted with a loud snap. The Indian yelped in pain, the string lashing about and cutting his hand.

Distracted, the Crow hunter was no match for the Trailsman. Fargo jabbed with his left and then kicked hard to knock the brave's leg out from underneath him. The Indian crashed to the ground, stunned. A second blow on the side of the head knocked the man out.

Panting, Fargo looked down to be sure the Indian wasn't playing possum. The hunter was unconscious, so Fargo could set out on the trail after Carstairs again.

Sheathing his knife, he loped along in the direction taken by the undertaker. Fargo settled into a ground-devouring pace he could keep up all day, if necessary. He overtook Carstairs just as the undertaker reached the lake.

"Hold on!" Fargo cried.

"No, you'll kill me!" shrieked Carstairs. He floundered about in knee-deep water before stepping on something slippery and falling into the water. Carstairs thrashed about and started swimming for the middle of the lake. Fargo had no idea what the man intended on doing. If he thought to reach one of the distant desert islands and reestablish himself in exile, self-imposed this time, he was wrong.

Fargo drew his six-gun and fired in front of the swimming man. A tiny plume of water rose as the hot lead tore into the saltwater lake.

"Get back here," Fargo called, "or the next one will send you to the bottom for good. No man can swim with a belly full of lead!"

Carstairs reluctantly returned. He came from the water with his hands high above his head. Wet, naked, and bedraggled, he was a funny sight, but Fargo was not laughing.

"I'm turning you over to Marshal Gutherie. He'll know what to do with you."

"I'll tell you where the watch is if you let me go. You don't even have to give me any clothes or anything. Just let me go."

"In a pig's eye," Fargo said. "How do I know you won't lie to me?"

"I'm an honest man."

"You're not even an honest thief. I can understand a man risking his neck to hold up a stage or to rob a bank. There's a chance he might get ventilated by a guard or a shotgun messenger, but he takes the risk anyway. The only people you ever robbed were already dead and couldn't fight back. Start walking."

Fargo found his Ovaro and mounted. He marched the naked undertaker all the way back to Great Salt Lake City.

12

Fargo created quite a stir as he rode into Great Salt Lake City, herding the naked undertaker ahead of him. As he passed tight knots of wide-eyed, open-mouthed citizens, silence would fall. After he rode on, noisy gossip ran wild in the crowds. Children dashed all about to tell everyone they could about the Trailsman returning with the most infamous man in town.

"This isn't right. It's downright indecent," protested Carstairs, trying to hide his privates from sight with his hands and not succeeding. Women in the crowd averted their eyes, but Fargo saw many covering their mouths to hide snickering. It served the undertaker right. Fargo counted this indignity as part of Carstairs's punishment. What else Marshal Gutherie and the judge might do because of the undertaker's escape from Frémont Island remained to be seen, but right now some justice was being served.

"Hush up," Fargo said in response to Carstairs's whining. "We've only got another mile before we get to the courthouse."

"I know what happened to the watch. I'll tell you. Let me go. I beg you!"

Fargo understood the Crows' contempt for the man's weakness. He appeared emotionless most times, but when his feelings did come out, they gushed like a mountain stream during spring runoff.

"The Crow destroyed the watch. You've got nothing to trade for your freedom with me, Carstairs."

"They took it from me!" The man sounded frantic.

"Of course, they did. I know that already. You're lucky those Indians didn't take your scalp, too."

"No, not the Indians. The others. I'll tell you if you'll let me go."

"Too late," Fargo said, seeing Marshal Gutherie riding up fast. Two deputies trailed behind him. Good news traveled fast.

"They'll lynch me. If you help me, I'll tell you everything!"

"Fine—I won't let them hang you," Fargo said, the words burning on his tongue. "Now start spilling."

"Th-the watch. It was stolen by the two men who took me to Frémont Island. They stole everything of value I had and left me with only the clothes on my back."

"Which you managed to lose to the Crows," Fargo said, appreciating the irony of the situation. A man who had robbed the dead of their fine duds now walked naked.

"You won't let them hurt me?" Carstairs turned, his eyes wide with fear. "They did terrible things to me when I was in jail. The desert island was almost a relief."

"I reckon you have more terrible things in store in your future," Fargo observed. Gutherie reined back hard. His horse's hooves dug into the street and sent up a spray of gravel that pelted Carstairs's bare flesh and made the man wince.

"You found the son of a bitch. I got word he had escaped the island after one of my deputies took supplies out to him."

"The Crows did this to him," Fargo explained. "They tortured him a mite before I convinced them to let him go in my custody." Fargo's icy blue eyes locked on Gutherie's. "I had to promise nothing would happen to him that wasn't sanctioned by your law."

"They made you promise that, did they?" Gutherie glared at Fargo, knowing none of it was true. "Well, I'm not gonna do anything to him the judge doesn't order."

"Lock him up," Fargo said. "Do that and I'll be happy when I come check on him in a day or two."

"What's stuck in your craw, Fargo? He don't deserve your protection."

Fargo looked at the cringing Carstairs and said, "I know. But he's got it. For the time being." Fargo waited to see if the undertaker wanted to change his story. It was clear from Fargo's tone that, if Carstairs lied, he was going to be thrown to the wolves. Being caught by the Crows might have been a more merciful end.

"I'm not lying," Carstairs called as the two deputies tossed ropes around him and led him toward the jailhouse like a calf to a branding. "I'm telling the truth, Fargo!"

"What's that about?" asked Gutherie.

"Nothing that concerns you, Marshal," said Fargo. "When are Lamont and the Utah Kid going on trial?"

"Well, now, that's something of a problem. They're singing like waterthrushes, blamin' Les Schatten for about everything, including locust, last year's drought, and Zeke Smith's bull jumpin' the fence. Doesn't seem right tryin' them without Schatten, too."

"He hightailed it?" Fargo wasn't surprised. The politician had to realize the danger in staying in town to stand trial.

"Let's just say he's makin' himself mighty scarce. I didn't think lettin' him out on bail was such a bad idea, because I wanted to see who he talked to. I figured he wasn't the only crooked politician in town. But he's gone to ground."

"He's left town?"

"I doubt that he got far, if he did leave this fair city. No, I suspect he's hidin' out around here. I got my boys huntin' for him. Schatten's smart as a weasel and half as trustworthy. He'll stay close, where people owe him favors."

"He paid Lamont to kill 'Rone. Both Lamont and the Utah Kid say so."

"I believe them. Reckon the judge does, too, but the trial's postponed until we find Schatten." Marshal Gutherie smiled crookedly. "This is a double pleasure. Never much liked Schatten, and now I get to keep the money he posted for his bond."

"I want to see Schatten swing for the crime," Fargo said. As Gutherie turned to head back to the jailhouse with his prisoner, Fargo called after him. "Who rowed Carstairs out to Frémont Island?"

The marshal glanced back over his shoulder, frowned, and shook his head. "Don't rightly remember their names. I left that up to my chief deputy, because I'd've sent Carstairs straight to the bottom of the lake with that ball and chain fastened around his neck."

"See that no harm comes to him now," Fargo warned. He wondered if Carstairs was flapping his tongue to keep himself alive, or if he had told the truth about the two men robbing him.

It was something Fargo had to look into later. Right now he wanted to talk with Lydia and let her know what had happened over the past few days. He rode slowly to the edge of town where her neat, whitewashed house stood. As before, the steps leading to the front door seemed to stretch forever.

The fact that he was always bringing bad news had something to do with it, but he knew there had to be more.

"Skye!" Lydia rushed from inside the house, having seen him through the side window. She threw her arms around his neck and kissed him hard when his feet touched ground. The Ovaro whinnied and shied a mite, but Fargo did not. It felt good having Lydia's soft, supple flesh in the circle of his arms once more. Better than he would have thought.

"Why so glum?" she asked. "What have you been up to? I've missed you so much!" She bubbled over with excitement at seeing him again. He wished he had the watch for her, but at least he hadn't promised her outright. He had just thought it was a good way to discharge his promise to 'Rone before moving on.

"I've got quite a story to spin for you," he told her.

"I want to hear every word of it. You were gone so long, I thought you had abandoned me. I'm not sure how I could have gone on, if you had." She smiled brightly and stared lovingly into his blue eyes. "Come inside," she said, taking his hand as they went up the steps. Fargo felt suddenly exhausted. Every step weighed down like a ton on his shoulders. He almost collapsed on the love seat in the parlor.

"You look plumb tuckered out," Lydia said, sitting beside him. She ran her fingers up his arm. When he winced, she pushed back his shirtsleeve to reveal the crudely bandaged cut on his left arm. "What happened?"

Fargo told of his chase after Carstairs, of the Crow chief and the fight, of returning the undertaker to Marshal Gutherie's custody.

"He was naked?" she said, smiling. Then Lydia laughed with real glee. "You brought him back naked, for everyone to see? How humiliating that must have been for him."

"It was. I couldn't bring myself to leave him with the Crows or shoot him myself, so it was the best I could do."

"It was perfect, Skye, simply perfect! Real retribution for his crimes. But I really don't know why you took it on yourself to recapture him, or why you went out to the island in the first place."

Fargo started to tell her of his plan to get 'Rone's watch for her, but he didn't get that far. Lydia moved closer, so that her leg rubbed against his on the love seat. Her lips parted slightly and her brown eyes closed. Fargo accepted the silent invitation by kissing her hard.

Their lips crushed passionately. Lydia turned in the seat so her breasts pressed into Fargo's chest. He felt himself responding to her beauty, to her passion, to the desires burning inside him. Fargo reached up and brushed strands of brunette hair away from her face, then kissed her closed eyes, nibbled at her earlobe, licked and kissed the back of her neck. Each time he moved on he excited Lydia that much more.

He stroked her long, lustrous hair and reveled in its silky feel under his fingers. Lydia turned her face up to his, begging to be kissed. He obliged her. Their lips touched, a feathery soft contact more like a falling snowflake than a passionate kiss. Her hot breath gusted out across his lips and cheeks. With a pecking motion, he pressed his lips to hers with more desire.

"Yes, Skye, I'm so glad you're back. You do so much for me. You would never let me down, would you?"

"No," he said, silencing her with a more ardent kiss. His hands moved over her cheeks and down her neck, dancing lightly across her bare arms. Lydia turned slightly, grabbed his wrist and moved it to her chest. He felt the excited hammering of her heart beneath as he squeezed down her breast.

Lydia swung about on the love seat and hiked one leg over his so she could rub her most intimate region against his thigh. Rocking back and forth slowly, the woman aroused herself more and more as Fargo felt his own pulse racing ever faster.

He felt as if he had it all. His hand was filled with a firm, warm breast, his mouth was locked to Lydia's in a blazing kiss that took away his breath, and she pressed herself down ardently on his leg. Every movement now, no matter how slight, pushed both of them upward to the heights of desire.

He reached around her trim body and pulled her closer until their chests rubbed as amorously as his leg did against her hidden nether lips. They stayed locked this way only for a moment. Lydia rolled to one side so she could tempt him with new delectations of the flesh.

"Oh, Skye, I can't stand it. I want more. I want you!"

He began kissing her throat, then moved lower. Button by button, he opened her blouse until her milky-white breasts tumbled free. Catching one cherry-red nipple between his lips, he sucked hard. Fargo thought she was going to explode then and there.

He held her tightly and bore her to the floor. Lydia moaned loudly and thrashed about under him as he continued to suckle at her breast. His tongue lashed out against the pulsing, hard cap of sensitive flesh and then pressed it downward, teasing it. Lydia's chest heaved as air gusted in and out of her lungs.

"I feel weak all over, Skye. You thrill me, baby. Now give me even more!"

"Like this?" he asked, applying his mouth once more to her surging breasts. He buried his face between those creamy mounds. He licked and nipped and sucked, heightening the sensations roiling within the amorous woman.

Fargo felt a growing urgency in his own loins. He hurriedly pushed aside Lydia's blouse and fumbled to unfasten the hooks and buttons of her skirt. The woman arched up off the floor, allowing Fargo to scoot her skirt away from her waist. She kicked the unwanted clothing away when he got it down around her long, sleek legs.

Fargo stared at her naked glory for a moment, like a kid in a candy store. Her body stretched before him was simply perfect—well proportioned, supple, and quivering with lust. He hardly knew what to do next.

"Get naked, Skye," she breathed huskily. "Go on. I'll be right back." Fargo watched as she suddenly got to her feet and lithely ran toward the kitchen. He unfastened his gun belt and kicked out of his boots. Stripping off his buckskins left him clad only in his long underwear. He had just pulled it down when a beautiful, deliciously naked Lydia returned.

"Here," she said.

"Honey?"

"Dribble this over me. Then lick it off!"

The sultry brunette lay down again on the floor, stretching her arms high over her head and arching up like a cat basking in the sun. Her breasts flattened slightly by the action, then came back into full relief when she relaxed.

"Go on," she urged. Fargo did as she requested, using a honey dripper to leave a thick golden trail all over her breasts and throat and then down to her belly.

Fargo began licking avidly, the sweetness of the honey mingling with the taste of an aroused woman. By the time he worked down to the deep depression of her belly button, he was straining and achingly erect.

"My turn," she said as he started to work lower, to the fleecy triangle hidden between her legs.

"But I was just getting to the interesting part," Fargo protested.

"I'll show you interesting," she promised, taking the honey dripper and letting viscous strands of honey run down his stiffened pole. Before the honey trickled down his full length, she pounced on his manstalk, taking it entirely into her mouth.

Fargo gasped as her tongue roved up and down the most sensitive portions of his manhood. When he was certain he could not stand one more loving stroke of her darting tongue or the tickling rivulet of honey down his shaft, she backed away.

"Your turn again," Lydia said, propping herself up on her elbows. She lifted her knees and parted her legs, wantonly exposing herself. "And it's not your mouth I want now. You're hung like a stallion, Skye. Do what we both want."

He moved closer, positioning himself at the vee of her legs. Lydia lay flat on the floor, staring up at him with burning eyes. Her chest rose and fell rapidly as she panted and moaned. When Fargo reached down to part her nether lips with his fingers, she cried out.

"Yes, there, there. Oh, yes!"

Fargo scooted forward so that the head of his shaft rested in the hot crevice. He wiggled his hips around to situate himself, then sank forward easily into her steamy depths.

The smooth insertion took away Lydia's breath and almost cost Fargo his control. One instant he was out in the cool air. The next he was surrounded by clinging, gripping flesh.

He thought he had found paradise. When Lydia began working hidden inner muscles, massaging his buried length, Fargo gasped.

"You're so big in me, Skye! So big you fill me up. Now move, damn you, move!" Lydia lifted her rump off the floor and ground her hips down into his groin, as if she could take him even deeper into her most intimate niche.

Supporting his weight on his arms on either side of her sleek body, Fargo began moving in and out, quickly and easily finding the age-old rhythm of loving a woman. The heat in his loins and body grew faster then as Lydia quivered and struggled and strove for ever more beneath him.

A quick bursting rush signaled an end to the lovemaking, but neither of them was disappointed. Tired and sweaty, they stared into each other's eyes for a time, then silently rolled over and lay wrapped in the other's arms.

"It was good, Skye, the best," Lydia said after a spell. "No man has ever made me feel so good. You've never let me down, Skye. Ever."

Fargo did not answer. She was right. The lovemaking was the best, but he felt he had let her down by not finding 'Rone's watch. He had avoided telling her the purpose of going to Frémont Island had been to retrieve the timepiece, and he was glad. She would be disappointed in him and his abilities if he admitted how woefully he had failed.

He held her a little closer, but she wanted none of it at the moment. Lydia pushed away so she could look at him.

"What did you promise 'Rone as he was dying?"

The question took him by surprise. Of all the things he expected her to say at this moment, this was not it.

"I told him I'd look after you," Fargo said.

"You are doing a wonderful job!" Lydia stroked over his bare chest. When she found a sticky spot of honey she had missed before, she pounced on it.

Fargo felt a pang of guilt. Lydia wanted so little, and making her happy by surprising her with 'Rone's watch would mean so much to her. Fargo drifted as her lips touched him here and there, his thoughts more on Carstairs. The undertaker had probably told the truth when he said the men taking him to Frémont Island took the watch from him. They wouldn't tell anyone right away how they had robbed the grave robber, but they'd think of the watch as a trophy. With Fargo bringing Carstairs back to Great Salt Lake City the way he had, this would be the perfect time for them to start bragging about how they were the first to humiliate him.

"That feels mighty good, Lydia, but I have business to tend to," he said.

She mumbled something he did not understand. Then she moved her mouth to a spot where he did understand—again. Fargo decided he could chase down Gutherie's head deputy and learn from him who the men were who had rowed Carstairs to the island later.

13

Fargo tried to get in to see Marshal Gutherie, but the lawman had his hands full dealing with the irate citizens who wanted to lynch Carstairs. News of the naked return of the undertaker had spread throughout Great Salt Lake City faster than a prairie fire. The marshal halfheartedly turned the protesting citizens away, obviously wanting to toss aside his badge and join the crowd.

Fargo drifted around the jailhouse door, bumped and pushed by the boisterous mob, until he realized the furor was not going to die down anytime soon. The marshal was occupied with a portly man of some means and obvious importance and would be for some time. Gutherie's deputies were no more inclined to let Fargo in than any of the other men demanding to see Carstairs.

Changing his tactics, Fargo began the hunt for any of the marshal's deputies out in town. It took almost a half hour before he found a stout man wearing a badge gulping down an early dinner at a small restaurant. Fargo pulled up a chair and sat across from the man. The deputy looked at him with a gimlet eye.

"You're the one what brought Carstairs back," the deputy finally said, shoveling food in and hardly chewing before he swallowed. " 'Scuse me. I got to get back on patrol. The marshal's a real stickler for keeping the peace, specially now."

"I know how it is," Fargo said, looking down at the man's licked-clean plate. "He's always rushing around doing things and telling folks like you to do even more. Like the two deputies who rowed Carstairs out to Frémont Island."

"What 'bout them?"

"I wanted to thank them for their fine work," Fargo lied. "The trouble is, I don't know their names."

"They're not deputies. Hellman found them lounging around on the dock down at the lake."

"Hellman's the chief deputy?" Fargo grinned when the man nodded briskly. This deputy was obviously in a powerful hurry to get back to work. "Where might I find him?"

"Hellman? Can't say. Might be around the docks. With all the commotion in town since you brought that varmint back, Hellman might be over at the jail or the courthouse."

"With, uh, what were their names again?" Fargo fished for the information he needed. Finding Chief Deputy Hellman would not be necessary if he learned the names of the men who had taken Carstairs to his exile.

"The two gents what rowed Carstairs out to the island? That'd be Rollie King and Greenwood. But they don't need thankin'. They got paid fifty cents each for the chore. See you." With that the deputy was up and away, still stuffing a hunk of bread into his mouth as he left. Out in the street again on duty, the deputy hitched up his gun belt, then strutted away.

Fargo had the two names without tracking down Gutherie's chief deputy. He sat in the restaurant for a moment, wondering if his time was better spent ordering a meal and gobbling it down as the deputy had done or finishing his quest to retrieve 'Rone's watch. He was tiring quickly of Great Salt Lake City, in spite of its clean streets, neat houses, impressive buildings, and most gracious hospitality. The town was prosperous and its citizens law-abiding, which was what made Carstairs's crimes so much more terrible. If he did have to stay in a city, this one certainly had its appeals.

But the bustle was too much for him. There were too many people, all clamoring for his attention. Everything was too crowded, and he missed the wide open spaces, mountaintops, and grassy meadows that stretched to the far horizon. He wanted forests and a good hunt, along with the sense of freedom that being in the mountains gave him.

Fargo left to hunt for King and Greenwood. The quicker he tracked down 'Rone's watch so he could give it to Lydia, the sooner he could mount his Ovaro and ride for the sunset. Or the sunrise. Or in any direction that took him away from the frantic activity of a boomtown like Great Salt Lake City.

The activity along the dock area was at a minimum by the time Fargo got there. He wondered if there was anything but ferry travel around the shoreline. Fishing was out of the question in the lake due to the incredible amount of salt in the water, Fargo guessed. That left the men who ran larger boats ferrying passengers to different points around the lake—and exiled prisoners like Carstairs on the desert islands dotting the center of the lake.

"Hey, Greenwood, lend me a hand, will you?" called a man struggling to beach a rowboat. "I got a hole in the bottom."

Fargo stepped up to see who responded. A young man no older than twenty hurried over to help wrestle the row boat ashore. He knelt down with the other man as they examined the hull, then hastened off to fetch his own tools. Fargo stayed back and watched as Greenwood labored to patch the hole, wanting to gather up as much information as he could before he approached the young man. By the time Greenwood had finished, the sun was sinking down over the far end of the lake.

"Thanks," the older man said, shaking Greenwood's hand. "You're a godsend. Give my regards to your ma and pa."

"I certainly will, sir." Greenwood looked as if he was torn about what to do next. He glanced at the sunset, then picked up his tools and went to another boat. Fargo watched as the young man took another forty-five minutes to finish repairs here before wiping his hands on a tattered rag and setting off.

Fargo started to approach the man and strike up a conversation, but hesitated when two other men, about Greenwood's age, darted from an alley and walked on either side of him. Fargo was too far away to hear what they were saying, but from their furtive manner, he knew it was no good. Greenwood made a few obvious objections, shook his head, then seemed to reluctantly agree to whatever the others proposed. Greenwood hurried on, leaving the other two behind.

Picking up the pace, Fargo was ready to greet Greenwood when the young man dropped his tools outside a house and went inside. The low illumination from a kerosene lamp showed Greenwood hugging a woman and then hurrying out back to wash up. Fargo felt like a bounder for spying on Greenwood, but after the meeting with the other two men on the street he decided to be cautious and bide his time.

Greenwood was up to something. If he had taken 'Rone's watch off Carstairs, Fargo might find what else the young man did with his time.

Fargo wished he had taken the opportunity to eat at the restaurant earlier in the day. He was forced to watch Greenwood and his family—his mother, father and two siblings—eat what smelled to be a mighty fine dinner. For two cents he would have left the young man to what seemed an ordinary evening with his upstanding family. But the two men earlier in the day and the shifty talk kept Fargo where he was.

He had learned patience hunting in the mountains. Like the Crow, he could sit for hours, waiting for precisely the right moment to strike. When game was scarce, the wait might be an entire day. At least Fargo knew he wouldn't wait that long with young Greenwood.

Nodding off only to come awake at every faint noise kept Fargo on edge until almost midnight. His heart pounded when he saw Greenwood sneaking from the house, looking like a thief in the night. The young man looked back over his shoulder as if he feared he was being followed.

Fargo knew he was on to something when Greenwood did not head for the outhouse but instead turned and crept into town.

Great Salt Lake City lay as quiet as a grave this time of night. Fargo heard a deputy patrolling one street over. When Greenwood heard the slow pacing footsteps, he ducked into a doorway, cloaked in deep shadow.

He had to be up to no good to act this suspiciously.

When the deputy's footsteps faded away, Greenwood came out of the shadowy doorway like a timid prairie dog and looked around. Fargo expected him to dive back for cover at any instant, but the man's resolve hardened, and he strode off rapidly. Following him was more difficult in the city than it would have been in a forest, but Fargo was up to the chore.

Thoughts of recovering 'Rone's watch and perhaps turning a thief over to Marshal Gutherie ran through Fargo's head as he trailed behind the young man. Repeatedly Greenwood looked over his shoulder as if expecting to see the demons of hell hot on his heels. Fargo expertly avoided detection until Greenwood reached an abandoned house near the shore of the salt lake.

He ducked inside. Fargo waited until the other two men showed up, like he knew they would, looking as sneaky as Greenwood. A faint light leaked through the broken boards in the walls. Going closer, Fargo pressed his eye against one rotting plank to see the three inside sitting around a guttering candle. One reached into his pocket and took out something he placed in the center of their circle.

Fargo decided it was time to join the party. He walked around to the door, put his hand on his Colt, then kicked in the door. It exploded off its hinges, rotted wood tearing away from the metal hinges. He followed quickly.

"Don't move, any of you!" he called out.

"Don't shoot!" Greenwood cried. "We didn't mean to do it. We—"

"Shut up," said another of the trio. "This ain't the law. Hell, he ain't even one of our parents or an elder."

Fargo stepped closer and saw what had been in the bag. Shreds of tobacco were scattered on the floor. All three had been rolling cigarettes. A half-empty bottle of whiskey sat to one side.

"You're not thieves, are you?" Fargo asked. Then he laughed. "You're sneaking out here to smoke and drink."

"That's our business, mister," Greenwood said, getting some of his courage back. Or maybe it was just Dutch courage from taking a few swigs of the whiskey. "You're not going to tell our folks, are you?"

"Why should I?" Fargo relaxed and went to where the three sat, tense as rabbits with a wolf on the prowl. "You're grown men. Why are you sneaking around like this?"

"You don't understand. It's a sin to smoke and drink," Greenwood said. He glared at his friend and added, "And to cuss."

"So you come here, roll a smoke and drink a shot or two, then go home? No women?"

"Certainly not!" Greenwood was outraged. "There are no loose women in Great Salt Lake City."

Fargo didn't bother pointing out the obvious. If they found tobacco and whiskey in the Mormon community, they could also find soiled doves. He picked up the whiskey bottle, motioned to Greenwood for permission, and then took a healthy swig.

"How'd you come to like the taste of whiskey and tobacco?" he asked, curious.

"We all went out on our year of missionary work to other parts of the Great Salt Lake Valley. Out there, things are not quite as . . . pious."

"So you brought back your bad habits." Fargo heaved a sigh. "I don't reckon you know anything about the watch Carstairs had on him when you rowed him out to Frémont Island?"

Greenwood sat a little straighter. From the set to his jaw and the way his lips thinned, he knew a great deal.

"Rollie took the undertaker's watch. I argued with him about it. But Rollie didn't see it my way and took it before we chained Mr. Carstairs and left."

"You wouldn't steal anything, would you?" asked Fargo.

"No, sir, I would not."

Fargo believed him.

Silence fell as Fargo considered what he had to do if he wanted the watch back. Then he nodded to the young men and turned to go.

"Wait a minute," Greenwood called out. "You're not going to squeal on us, are you?"

"I wouldn't know who to tell," Fargo said honestly. He tossed the bottle onto the floor near Greenwood. "Enjoy yourselves."

He left the three young men whispering among themselves like conspirators ready to perpetrate the greatest crime imaginable. Fargo shook his head in wonder. Maybe for them smoking and drinking and cussing fit the bill.

For him, what Carstairs did was a lot worse. Fargo went to find Rollie King and set things right.

14

Fargo was bone tired from watching a man, hardly more than a boy, trying to sneak out and indulge in a few vices frowned upon by his family and religion. He wondered if tracking down Rollie King was likely to gain him the watch, since his luck was turning bad.

Fargo rode slowly back toward Lydia's house, considering what he ought to do. His promise to 'Rone had not explicitly mentioned the watch. All he had promised his dying partner was to see to Lydia. He had taken it into his head she should have the watch as a keepsake because she found 'Rone's ring less than desirable after Carstairs had worn it. It might be time to get it off his chest what he intended, rather than trying to surprise her. At least, that was the lie he told himself.

He wanted to do more than report his progress to her, and the watch was only an excuse to stay around. Lydia Pressman was the single thing keeping him in Great Salt Lake City, and he used this scavenger hunt for 'Rone Clawson's watch as an excuse to keep sampling her charms. It was late at night, but Fargo doubted the woman would mind too much if he showed up at her front door, especially after the last time together.

Leaving her would be the hardest thing he would do, but the call of the wide-open spaces sounded more and more agreeable to him. He wasn't meant to stay in a city long, and he had been here for what seemed an eternity already.

Fargo reined back when he saw a light burning in Lydia's window. A little smile danced on his lips. He wouldn't even have to wake her. Then he saw a saddled horse tethered at the side of the house. He frowned. She had a nocturnal visitor. He rode slowly, approaching the front of the house, then dismounted.

Fargo was afraid of what he might find. He hesitated, as he had before, then was startled when Lydia opened the door and rushed out onto the porch. She had a robe pulled tightly around her. Her pale face was flushed, and she seemed excited.

"I heard you ride up, Skye. What is it?"

"You busy?"

"I—no, not at all. Come in. Please. Hurry, though. I don't want people seeing me entertaining you this late at night."

As Fargo took the three steps to the porch, he heard the horse at the side of the house whinny. He paused, hand resting on the butt of his Colt.

"Skye, what's wrong?" Lydia came to him quickly, her warm hand pressing into his on the six-shooter. "Come in."

He started to ask who her visitor was, then heard the soft plodding of hooves as her unknown guest rode away.

A bit louder than necessary—to cover her visitor's retreat?—Lydia said, "I was thinking about you. I have been worrying about how you've been taking off for hours and hours, and that maybe you wouldn't come back to me."

Fargo let himself be led inside. Lydia sat, clutching her robe tighter around herself. She chose a chair across from the couch where Fargo sank down tiredly.

"It's nice to know you've missed me. I've got some unfinished business and won't leave until it's resolved. Do you know a man named Rollie King?"

Her response puzzled Fargo. She jumped as if he had stuck her with a pin, then she tried to cover her agitation. "I'm not sure. The name is familiar. Great Salt Lake City is not that large a place."

"But large enough so you don't know everyone?"

"That's so," she said, fiddling with her robe's belt. "Skye, I don't want to seem ungrateful, but could I ask you to go? I'm feeling a bit under the weather."

"You looked flushed when you came to the door," he said. "Are you sure you don't know Rollie King? He was one of the men who rowed Carstairs out to the island."

"Please, Skye, it is late," she said in a voice that might

as well have come from a thousand miles away. Lydia gave him a quick kiss and herded him quickly toward the door.

As he mounted his Ovaro and rode off, he wondered who her visitor had been. Some lover she wanted to keep hidden from him? Fargo had caught a glimpse of her naked breasts and the tangled bush of nut-colored fleece between her legs when she first came out of the house. Or was it more innocent than that? Perhaps she did not wear a night-gown when she slept. The night was warm, and Fargo knew nothing about Lydia and her personal habits.

It didn't pay to dwell too much on what was and what wasn't when he knew so little. Fargo knew he ought to ride on, find a place to spend the night and get to Rollie King at first light. But he found himself circling Lydia's house and hunting for the tracks left by the mysterious rider. Fargo used the faint moonlight to follow the hoofprints until clouds blowing over the lake blotted out the illumination.

Dropping to the ground, he walked along leading his horse. This permitted him to keep the tracks in view. For a half hour he followed the trail as it led out of town and into the foothills of the desert bowl holding both Great Salt Lake City and the lake. Then the rider rode across rocky patches that muddled the trail and forced Fargo to spend more time locating the hoofprints.

By dawn he had lost the trail completely. Fargo looked around, trying to guess which way the rider had gone. He had hightailed it directly from Lydia's house to the forested area outside town, making no stops, with no hesitation about his route. That meant the rider had a definite destination in mind.

"A hideout," Fargo decided. He could search the woods for a month and never find who had paid Lydia such a late-night visit. He could not resolve the real question troubling him most. Was she seeing someone else, or was this other business that he knew nothing about?

As he rode back to town, Fargo wondered if Lydia would give him a straight answer if asked outright. He doubted it, since she had not ventured any explanation the night before and had done what she could to hide her visitor's departure.

Fargo shrugged it off. He was making a mountain out of

a molehill. She was getting on with her life. Fargo knew what he had to do: recover 'Rone's watch, discharge what he thought of as his promise to his partner by giving it to Lydia, then leave for country more to his liking. The desert around the lake was beginning to wear on him as the heat mounted during the day, only to leave the night downright chilly.

Returning to the dockside area afforded him the best chance of finding Rollie King. Or so he thought. Fargo spent an hour asking after the man, only to find few willing to talk with him.

A merchant two blocks away from the docks where a ferry took passengers to various points around the lakeshore told Fargo, "I don't deal with that son of a bitch anymore." The man, missing a front tooth and old enough to have fought in the Revolutionary War, looked around to see if anyone but Fargo had overheard. "Sorry 'bout that. Folks in these parts don't cotton much to swearin'."

"But Rollie King is enough to make you cuss a blue streak?" asked Fargo.

"Stole me blind, he did. I gave him a job, and he made off with anything not nailed down. And the things that were, well, he just stole the nails before making off with the goods."

"When was the last time you saw him?"

"Don't see him much at all these days. He avoids me like the grippe. Knows I'll ram a boat hook into his worthless guts if I do see him."

"Deputy Hellman thought enough of him to hire him to take Carstairs out to Frémont Island."

"Hellman," snorted the merchant. "If brains was gunpowder, he couldn't blow his nose. Always lookin' for the easy way out. He ought to have taken that thievin' coyote out to the island himself, but he figgered to hire it out."

"The Greenwood boy seems honest enough."

"If I know King, he hired Greenwood to do all the rowin' while he watched the prisoner. Wouldn't do a lick of work himself, that Rollie King. Heard tell he's fallen in with bad company, too."

"How's that?"

"Gossip, that might be all it is, but people are sayin' King's been seen talkin' to Gus Lamont."

"Since Lamont was jailed?" Fargo read the answer on the man's grizzled face before he spoke.

"Before. They've been hangin' out together and actin' thicker 'n thieves." The man laughed at this. "Thieves surely does cover both of 'em, and both of 'em ought to be hung."

Fargo started to go, then paused. He asked. "Whose boat was it they used?"

"To get Carstairs out there so's he could escape? Reckon it was King's boat."

"Does he ferry passengers around like the others?" Fargo pointed to a barge heaving in to the dock.

"Never thought on it. He was always going out in that boat, and it wasn't no rowboat neither. A good-sized dinghy, it was." The old man closed one eye and peered at Fargo. "What you so all fired interested in King for? He owe you money? If you collect, don't forget old Jess. He owes me, too!"

"I'll remember," Fargo said, grateful for what the man had told him. Something about King owning a large boat figured into finding him, but Fargo could not get a hold of exactly how. Yet.

He spent the rest of the day asking after King and finding nothing but an undercurrent of contempt for the man. Unlike Old Jess, the people he spoke to were unwilling to say what they thought about Rollie King.

Whatever King was involved in, it had to be illegal. If King was mixed up with Lamont and the Utah Kid, the lawbreaking could involve something both in town and out. That meant Deputy Hellman might also be mixed up in it, since he had picked King to take Carstairs to Frémont Island. Fargo found the deputy late in the afternoon and trailed him, trying not to be conspicuous. If he had been in the mountains or even out on the plains, he could have watched without fear of being seen. Fargo was a superb woodsman and tracker, but in the city he had to make do with what buildings he came across to hide himself from the deputy.

Hellman made his rounds, talked a short while with Marshal Gutherie, then went off duty just after sundown. Fargo's feet were aching from so much walking, and his patience was wearing thin, but this was his best chance for finding King. If Rollie King was the cur everyone claimed, he seemed the least likely person in all of Great Salt Lake City for the deputy to hire for an important trip like taking Carstairs to Frémont Island.

The deputy had dinner at a small café, then came out rubbing his full belly and picking his teeth. Fargo's own stomach growled at him over the outrageous mistreatment of not feeding it, but his pulse pounded a little faster and he forgot his hunger when Hellman looked around, then started off purposefully for the lakeshore.

Hellman glanced over his shoulder occasionally, nothing too obvious, to be sure no one followed him. Fargo felt more at home now. He used low-growing bushes, scrubby trees, and the sandy, salty dunes along the lake for cover. The farther Deputy Hellman went, the more cautious he became. Fargo was certain now the deputy was up to no good.

When Hellman suddenly vanished from sight, Fargo had to make a quick decision. Close the gap and possibly be spotted, or lie back and wait?

He dashed across the sandy strand and rounded a large dune, heading away from the lake, slowing only when he heard angry voices. Fargo dropped to his belly and snaked forward so he could look over the dune crest. The deputy leaned against a stack of small wooden crates, staring at a man struggling to bring another up from a boat beached some distance away.

"Get your ass moving, Rollie. We ain't got all night."

"Some help would be appreciated, Hellman," complained the man lugging the heavy crate. He dropped it at the deputy's feet.

"Careful now. We don't want to break a single bottle."

"What's it to me? You're stealing all the money we get from selling this rotgut."

"Stealing is a mighty harsh word. You're paid for bringing it over from the far side of the lake."

"Not paid near enough," grumbled King. The man sat on a crate and pried open another. He took out a bottle. From where Fargo spied on the two men, he recognized the shape and contents right away. Hellman and King were smugglers, bringing in illicit liquor to sell to men like Greenwood and his friends. Rollie King might have been the source of the firewater he had tasted the other night. That explained young Greenwood's reticence about discussing anything with him. If Fargo caught up with King and got him in trouble with the law, the river of illegal booze might dry up.

"You sayin' I've been cheatin' you?" The coldness in Hellman's voice hinted at a shoot-out. King seemed oblivious to how close to the edge he walked with the deputy.

"You surely don't pay me half of what I'm worth."

Fargo saw Hellman's hand twitch slightly, as if he was going to throw down on his partner in smuggling. Fargo could not let the deputy kill Rollie King, not until he recovered 'Rone's watch. King might carry it with him, but Fargo feared the worst. Men like King found that money turned to water in their grasp. If they had it, they spent it. And if King had taken the watch as Greenwood claimed, he had probably sold it by now.

The rattle of a heavy wagon forced Fargo back down behind the dune. He inched around and saw two others jump from the wagon and saunter onto the beach where the whiskey was stacked.

"Here it is, boys," said Hellman. "Get it loaded." He turned, squared his stance, and rested his hand on the handle of his six-gun. "After you pay up, naturally."

"You're a son of a bitch, Hellman," complained one burly freighter. "That's why I like you." He fumbled in his pocket and pulled out a wad of greenbacks thick enough to choke a cow.

Hellman took the money, counted it, then counted it again before nodding. The two men started loading the liquor on the wagon, shipping it to whoever sold it in Great Salt Lake City.

"Gimme my share now," King said. He put a bottle of whiskey down on the sand and held out his hand.

Again Fargo worried Hellman might gun down the smuggler, but the presence of the other two held the deputy's annoyance in check. He stripped off a few bills and passed them to King.

"Hey, you shorted me!"

"I deducted the amount of a bottle of that tarantula juice," Hellman said. "Be glad I didn't charge you what *they* charge their customers." He jerked his thumb back over his shoulder in the direction of the two men loading the last cases into their wagon.

"You ought to give me a bottle or two at least. That's a long trip across the lake, and it gets mighty lonely out there."

"I ought to . . ." Hellman shoved the money into his pocket and glared at his henchman. Fargo saw King wipe his forehead, then take a long pull from the bottle he had bought so dearly.

"Next time I'll steal it while I'm still out on the lake," King grumbled. "I knew I ought to have thrown in with Lamont and them others instead of lettin' you push me around. They made real money. Gold!"

"You worthless sot," Hellman sneered. "Gus and the Kid are in jail because they're stupid. You'd be with them, waiting to have your neck stretched, if I hadn't saved your hide and put you on to real money."

"He didn't have no map," King said, his words slurring more with every pull he took on the bottle. "And leaving that boat for him didn't pan out, either. The damned fool runs off and gets caught by Indians."

"You were supposed to be out on the lake and trailin' him," Hellman said. "Where were you when he got off the island?"

King turned furtive, took a drink and finally said, "I got me a woman. A right fine one, too. Can't blame me for bein' with her 'stead of freezin' my ass off out on the lake, waitin' for that corpse robber to get away."

"If you'd found the map, we wouldn't have needed to go to all that trouble."

"He didn't have no map on him, Hellman. Don't care if he stole everything from the dead."

"He surely didn't have a map on him when Fargo brought him back. All he had was a bad case of sunburn." The deputy laughed raucously and slapped King on the back, staggering the man. On unsteady legs, King turned and went toward his boat. Hellman rested his hand on the butt of his six-shooter, as if considering what trouble he would be in by shooting down the bootlegger.

Fargo tensed. He could not let Hellman gun down King. The deputy came to a decision, took his hand off his six-gun and walked off down the lakeshore, vanishing in a few seconds. The two freighters finally got their balky team to pull up the sandy beach and onto more solid ground, rattling away. Fargo swarmed up and over the dune to catch Rollie King before he got into his boat.

King heard the footsteps behind him and half turned in time to see Fargo charging at him. The man swung his bottle of whiskey and caught Fargo on the side of the head. The glancing blow caused him to stumble, but did not stop his forward progress. Crashing into King, Fargo tackled the man and drove him to the sandy beach.

"What's goin' on?" demanded King.

"Can't you guess?" Fargo said, pushing the man back flat to the sand and drawing his six-shooter.

"You're too late to steal my whiskey. They already carted it off."

"I don't want the damned whiskey."

"Here, take this," King said, fumbling with the money Hellman had paid him. Fargo knocked it from his hand, not even caring what the deputy thought the smuggling was worth.

"What do you want?" cried King. He stared down the barrel of Fargo's Colt. Then the man turned pale when the six-gun cocked. His mouth opened and closed like a beached fish. He made tiny trapped-animal squeaks as he struggled for words.

"I want the watch you took off the undertaker when you dumped him on Frémont Island."

"What?"

"Three seconds."

"Three seconds?"

"Until I blow your head off. Two."

"Wait, wait! I remember. I took a watch off Carstairs. What did he need it for, anyway? That kid with me thought it would be worse punishment if Carstairs was reminded what time it was every day in exile, but I figured I could sell the watch."

"So you sold it?"

"No, I didn't. But I don't have it, either."

"One," said Fargo, shoving the six-gun into King's mouth. "You've wasted all your time and haven't told me squat. Good-bye!"

Rollie King mumbled out something that made Fargo

pull the six-shooter back enough so the man could speak without having the iron barrel shoved into his tonsils.

"I didn't sell it. I . . . I lost it in a card game. I know we ain't supposed to gamble. Hell, we ain't supposed to smoke or drink neither, but folks do. They just do it on the quiet and—"

"Time's up." Fargo thrust the six-shooter forward again. He was tired of King's drunken rambling.

"I lost it in a stud-poker game to Silas! Silas Gentry. He took a real fancy to it and let me tear up markers for fifty dollars, the old fool."

"You won't be able to run far enough if you're lying to me," Fargo said, getting up. He shoved his six-shooter back into its holster and brushed the sand off his buckskins as he watched Rollie King scramble to get in his boat and shove off. The lake waters parted with a soft sigh as King's boat floated farther away.

Fargo watched the frightened smuggler leave, then picked up the whiskey bottle and took a long drink. He spat it out.

"All that work to smuggle it, and you might as well have bottled horse piss," he said to King's disappearing boat, tossing the bottle into the lake after the smuggler.

Rollie King had tried to throw in with Lamont and the Utah Kid, was smuggling booze for Deputy Hellman, and had robbed Carstairs. Fargo frowned, remembering what the deputy had said about them putting the leaky rowboat on Frémont Island so Carstairs could escape. King was supposed to have followed because they thought he had some kind of a map and they figured he would make a beeline for it. Fargo shook his head. All Carstairs had done was light out for the high country to get away from his punishment.

He had a lot to tell Marshal Gutherie the next time he saw him, but he had something more pressing to do first. Fargo set out to find Silas Gentry and recover 'Rone's watch. As he mounted the Ovaro he felt success was finally within his grasp.

15

Fargo thought it would be simple to find Silas Gentry, but he had not counted on the religious climate in Great Salt Lake City. No one wanted to admit knowing a gambler or being in a game with him, fearing public denunciation. Stretching his tired muscles from being in the saddle so long and squinting into the rising sun, Fargo wondered if he would ever get the watch back. He had looked after Lydia the best he could and giving her 'Rone's watch wasn't really necessary, but Fargo felt he would disappoint her if he didn't, although he had not actually promised her this simple legacy.

For all that, he had not actually promised 'Rone he would see she got it. Fargo had to be honest with himself as to why he stayed so long. There was a powerful lot of justice to be delivered to those responsible for 'Rone's death—and he certainly enjoyed nuzzling up against Lydia.

He rode slowly through the bustle and crush of an awakening city, finding himself back near the shore again. Old Jess put out his goods in front of his store and waved cheerily. If Fargo were a betting man, he would place all his money on Old Jess knowing Silas Gentry's whereabouts. Not much got past this eagle-eyed, sharp-eared merchant.

"Good morning," Fargo greeted.

"You're looking chipper. You must have found King. You get my money?"

Fargo closed his eyes as he remembered how he had knocked the wad of bills from King's hand and scattered the scrip all over the beach. Money didn't matter much to him, and he had not bothered to pick it up after King had shoved off and gotten his boat back onto the lake.

"Sorry, didn't think of it. I had other things on my mind at the time."

"I'll collect. Somehow, someday, that varmint'll pay up," Old Jess declared.

"I'm always amazed at what I find out about this town," Fargo said, dismounting. He helped Old Jess move a crate out to display stacks of rope suitable for use on boats plying the Great Salt Lake.

"The seamy underbelly?" Old Jess cackled when he saw he had hit the bull's-eye. "Most folks here are hardworking and God fearing and even religious by the strictest view."

"But a few aren't quite so hardworking, God-fearing and religious," Fargo said. "I found that out last night. Seems Deputy Hellman is responsible for smuggling a considerable amount of whiskey into town, and Rollie King is the boatman bringing it in for him from the other side of the lake."

"I'd heard some gents from Kain-tucky had a still over there." Old Jess cocked his head to one side and peered at Fargo. "The stuff's supposed to make you see double and think you're single."

"It's a wonder they can keep it corked," Fargo admitted. The bitter taste still lingered in his mouth. He wished he had some good whiskey to chase away the vile aftertaste.

"Yep, they came in from Kain-tuck so they could make their devil's brew and have themselves a couple wives. Nasty people."

"How nasty is Silas Gentry?"

"Silas? Why, he's a gentleman compared to them folks. A gamblin' man, true, but a gentleman nevertheless. You wantin' to find him now?"

Fargo said nothing. Old Jess took out a plug of tobacco, bit off a chaw, then offered it to Fargo. As tempted as he was, Fargo shook his head. Old Jess chewed in contentment for a minute, then spat accurately, hitting a bucket just inside the door.

"Folks look down on you dippin' snuff, chawin' terbacky and drinkin'. Me, I don't mind any of that. Even been known to gamble a mite." Old Jess studied Fargo, then added, "He's over at the barn behind the Smith place."

Fargo started off but Old Jess called after him, "Smith's a popular name in these parts. So's Joseph. Let me give you some directions." Old Jess detailed for Fargo the route

112

to the Smith's barn and the poker game he would find within that ran nonstop.

Finding the place proved easy enough, but Fargo immediately saw that getting in was going to be more difficult. Two men with rifles stood guard at the corners of the barn and another with a shotgun sat in the hayloft.

"Come to join in a hand or two," Fargo told the nearest man with a rifle.

"I don't know you." He checked with the other two, who shook their heads. "Nobody knows you. Get on out of here."

Fargo looked around. The farm appeared prosperous enough. A good-sized whitewashed wood farmhouse stood a few yards away. Crops in the field, clean, clear-running irrigation channels, fat chickens squawking noisily in the side yard and a dozen horses in the corral all showed how legitimate the place was. But Mr. Smith liked a game of chance and played poker in his barn.

"I need to talk to Silas Gentry. Just for a minute, then I'll clear out."

"Wait here." The rifleman ducked into the barn, returning a few minutes later with a dapper man, dressed to kill in a gray cutaway coat, brocade vest, and fancy pearl buttons. Fargo saw the dangling gold chain going from a buttonhole to a vest pocket. Gentry noticed his interest and pulled out the watch.

"Need to know the time, mister?"

"Not from that watch," Fargo said, seeing it was not 'Rone Clawson's. "I heard tell you had won a watch off Rollie King. It's a family keepsake I'd like to get back."

"King?" The gambler looked at the rifleman, who seemed disgusted. This was all the goad Gentry needed. "Oh, him. I took a watch from him. Worthless piece of tin, but it got rid of him. He was becoming a tad obstreperous." Silas Gentry let the last word roll off his tongue as if it were a fine wine.

"I'm willing to pay for that piece of tin," Fargo said.

"I normally would not consider such a matter," Gentry said, licking his lips, "but Lady Luck and I have been estranged for the better part of an hour."

"You have the watch?" Fargo's pulse raced.

"I do remember taking it in lieu of money," Gentry said, turning cagey. "What's it worth to you?"

Fargo knew the gambler would try to wrangle the best deal possible for something he cared nothing about.

"Does the watch still work?" Fargo asked. He saw Gentry turn irritable at this and knew the answer.

"It needs a bit of work, true, but other than this small item, it is in tip-top shape."

"One dollar," Fargo offered.

"Five and you have a deal," the gambler said. When Fargo hesitated, Gentry said, "I must return or lose my chance for a really good hand of seven-card stud. Make it two dollars."

"Done." Fargo fumbled in his shirt pocket and unfolded two rumpled dollar bills. Gentry made a face as if merely touching paper money was a chore, then reached out for it.

"Not so fast," Fargo said. "The watch, then the money."

"The money, hurry," Gentry said, glancing over his shoulder back into the barn. "They won't carry me much longer."

Fargo took the chance and let the gambler have the money. Gentry hurried back in, made his bet, and won the pot. He returned, smiling ear to ear.

"Fourteen dollars," he said with some satisfaction.

"That's fourteen dollars you wouldn't have won if I hadn't bankrolled you," Fargo pointed out. "The watch."

"Yes, yes, my good man. No need to get so antsy. Right away." Gentry walked to the corral and whistled. A paint that might have been a cousin to Fargo's Ovaro trotted over. Gentry dug in the saddlebags and came out with a watch Fargo remembered well, having last seen it in 'Rone Clawson's hands and reflecting light from a campfire somewhere outside Camp Floyd.

"That's the one," Fargo said. He opened it and saw the inside of the case had been scratched. He snapped shut the case, realizing no one who had held the watch was likely to have cared for it like 'Rone. "Much obliged."

"And I to you, sir," Gentry said. The gambler took out his meager winnings, looked back into the barn, then stuffed the greenbacks into his pocket. "A good gambler knows when to walk away."

"And you're a good one?" asked Fargo.

"No, I'm a great one. Good day, sir." With that Silas Gentry mounted his paint and trotted off, heading away from Great Salt Lake City. Fargo saw the three guards were getting itchy trigger fingers because he had not left. Fargo didn't want to give them an excuse to gun him down. He had no idea what the penalty for gambling in Mormon country was, but these men took it seriously. Fargo decided to, also.

He returned to town, pushing his Ovaro, since he wanted to deliver the watch to Lydia as quickly as possible. He reached her house about an hour later to find the same horse he had spotted before tethered in front of her house. Fargo instinctively made sure the pistol was riding easy in his holster and ready to draw. Hopping to the ground, he started up the steps, and when he reached the top step, he immediately went for his Colt when he saw who was awaiting him.

"Don't be foolish," Lester Schatten told him, his lip curling into a sneer. The politician slipped through the doorway, moving like a greased snake. "I don't have a six-shooter. You'd be committing murder."

"They'd never find the body," Fargo told him, his hand resting on the butt of his Colt. He hesitated when he saw a distraught Lydia right behind Schatten.

"Be seeing you," Schatten said, pushing past Fargo.

"In hell," Fargo replied, beginning to pull out his gun. Lydia frantically grabbed his wrist and kept him from gunning down the politician as he mounted his horse.

Schatten smirked, touched the brim of his hat, and rode off without another word.

"What was he doing here?" seethed Fargo. "He jumped bail. The marshal is willing to pay a good reward for him!" He tried to hold his temper in check. There was a great deal Lydia was not telling him, and that rankled him. Especially so, after he had gone to such trouble to retrieve 'Rone Clawson's watch to please her.

"He was just here to gloat," she said. "They've dropped all charges, and he wanted to tell me."

"What!" Fargo spun, drew, and aimed at the back of the retreating politician. The distance was too great—and Fargo knew he wouldn't pull the trigger and shoot the man in the back, anyway. He lowered the hammer and then angrily shoved the six-gun back into his holster.

"Lamont and the Utah Kid both have records here and

in Wyoming. Schatten convinced the judge they'd lie to save their own hides. With their testimony amounting to warm spit, there's nothing to tie Schatten to 'Rone's murder."

"He hired them to kill 'Rone," grumbled Fargo.

"I know. You know that, too, Skye, but the law's letting him go free. It's not right, but it's not for us to say. And it is certainly not for you to get into trouble over. Please." The lovely brunette laid her trembling hand on his arm. She was flushed and as pretty as a summer day.

"All right," Fargo said, hating the notion Schatten would not be tried. Maybe it was enough that Gus Lamont and his partner stood trial, but it didn't feel that way to him. Not right now.

"Come in. The day's starting to heat up something fierce."

He followed her in, noticing how disheveled she looked. Her hair floated in a fine mist around her head and her clothing was askew.

"Why was Schatten here the other night?" Fargo asked point-blank.

Lydia's eyes went wide. She swallowed, then averted her eyes as she answered. "He's been taunting me. He came here to mock me with how he had 'Rone killed. He's a terrible man. He's not like you, Skye, not honorable and kind and considerate."

"Why didn't you tell me?"

"What good would it do? Schatten is a powerful man in Great Salt Lake City. Look how easy it was for him to get all charges dropped."

It bothered Fargo that the woman had not confided in him rather than trying to deal with the slippery politician on her own.

"Maybe this will cheer you up," he said, reaching into his pocket to pull out 'Rone's watch. For a moment, Lydia simply stared as the timepiece twisted slightly on its cheap gold chain. Then she cried out in joy. It did Fargo's heart good to see her so happy again.

"You're wonderful, Skye. I thought it was lost forever!"

She hugged him tightly, then drew back just enough so she could turn her face to his. Brown eyes half closed and lips parted, she said in a husky whisper, "Your reward is waiting."

Before he could kiss her, Lydia pulled free and went toward the small bedroom. As she went, she unbuttoned her blouse and slipped one milky-white shoulder out of the garment. The other quickly followed. Then the unwanted clothing hit the floor. Lydia stood naked to the waist, her ample breasts swaying slightly in the warm summer-after-noon air. Capping each of those succulent globes rose cherry-red nipples, hardening in lust as Fargo watched.

"Don't keep me waiting," she said, turning away. As Lydia walked slowly to her bed, she unfastened her skirt and stepped out of it. The rest of her undergarments fell to the bedroom floor before she reached the bed. She looked over her shoulder and beckoned to Fargo. He saw a flash of her nut-brown mound, long white legs, and her bouncy bosom, all drawn together by the wanton look on her beautiful face. The sensual sight was more than he could —or wanted to—resist.

Fargo's lake-blue eyes fixed on her naked loveliness as he went into the bedroom, dropping his gun belt and working free of his unwanted clothing as he went. She sat on the edge of the bed, her legs spread just enough to give him hints of how wonderful his reward would be. As he kicked off his boots, Lydia hiked her feet to the bed, then spread her knees wide.

"See anything you want?" she asked coyly.

"Everything," he told her.

"It's all yours, Skye."

He dropped to the floor and buried his face in the fragrant bush between her legs. His tongue lapped out across her pink scalloped nether lips, then worked up toward her belly. Lydia moaned constantly now. Fargo felt the woman quivering beneath him, as eager as a racehorse ready to run.

He moved farther, his tongue dipping into the deep well of her navel. Then he worked farther north, finding the twin mounds of her breasts. He lavished kisses all over them, caught the throbbing buds cresting each one between his lips, and then used his teeth to nibble gently. Lydia's moans of passion grew louder and her movement beneath him wilder and less in control.

"You're driving me crazy, Skye. I'm on fire inside."

He did all he could to fuel that erotic fire. As he gobbled at her breasts, his hands slipped under her body and cupped her buttocks. Squeezing, gently at first and then harder and harder, he lifted her off the bed so her crotch pressed into his. As her softness touched his steel, he groaned with pleasure.

"I excite you, don't I?" she asked needlessly. He answered with his mouth, saving his words for later. His tongue lapped at one nipple and then the other. Then he sucked in as much of her left breast as he could. He felt the aroused woman's hammering heart only inches away through her soft mounds of flesh.

He released her and kissed his way up her throat to her wine-sweet lips. She began struggling then. Her hands roved over his broad back, stroking and stimulating him. When he lifted her off the bed again and ground his crotch into hers, Lydia's fingernails raked his bare flesh. Flame raced through his veins.

He felt himself pulsing hotly. Fargo moved his hips a little, then thrust forward. He buried himself deep into her yearning cavity. Lydia let out a shriek of unadulterated joy and clutched even more fervently at him. She began rotating her hips, stirring his thick rod around inside her.

Fargo gulped. It was getting harder and harder to hold back, but he wanted this to last as long as possible. She thrilled him more than any woman had in a long time. Every little twitch and tweak, every touch and scrape with her fingernails, the way her body responded, and the soft sounds of arousal all pushed him toward the edge of passion.

He felt himself boiling inside but held it back with iron control. It was too soon, but he was not sure how much longer he could withstand the sexual onslaught Lydia leveled against him.

The taste of her lips and breasts. The sweat beading her soft white skin. The way her legs locked around his waist, holding him firmly in place. Her tight wetness seemed to suck his resolve, beckoning him to bury himself deeper into her. He even reveled in the firmness of her rump as he kneaded the flesh as if it were twin mounds of bakery-fresh bread dough.

118

"You're huge inside me, Skye. But I need more. Move. Burn me up inside. Do it, I want it, oh, ohhh!"

He heeded her pleas because he could not stop himself. Fargo pulled back until the broad tip of his manhood parted her pink lips, paused a moment, then plunged back into her. He repeated this slow withdrawal and rapid entry with increasing need. Lydia gasped and sobbed and became incoherent with desire.

This pushed his own delight to new heights. His entire length was aflame now with the friction of his motion. Sounds mingled and thrilled him. The feel of the woman moving beneath him pushed him closer to the brink, but the sight of her was the real key. Lydia's eyes were screwed tightly closed, and her face was a mask showing ultimate elation.

Then she let out a cry of release. Her entire body shuddered like a leaf in a high wind as her tightness clamped down around Fargo's length like a collapsing mine shaft.

She gripped him powerfully, milking him. Fargo held on as her passion crested, then lost all hope of control. He began stroking faster, harder and deeper. She rocked on the soft bed, her knees pressing into either side of his body. He clung to her and levered himself forward. Heat built along his length, burning down into his core like a length of miner's fuse. When the heat hit his loins, he exploded like a keg of blasting powder.

He slammed forward, trying to split her apart with the power of his thrust. Lydia gasped again and again as she clutched at him like a fist in a velvet glove. He spewed into her hungering hollow as she writhed about under him.

He stroked hard until he felt himself beginning to melt like a winter icicle in the summer heat. Fargo sank down atop her, his chest pressing into hers. He kissed her and rolled to one side. Lydia clung to him and buried her face in his shoulder.

So softly he could hardly hear, she said, "Thank you, Skye, thank you for everything. I knew you would come through for me."

At that moment he would have traveled to the ends of the earth to fetch another watch for her, if it meant a repeat of this reward.

16

"You're going to leave, aren't you, Skye?" Lydia snuggled closer physically, but shied away emotionally. She knew what was in his mind better than he did.

"There's nothing for me in Great Salt Lake City," he told her.

"I'm here," she said in a small voice.

"You are," he admitted, "but there's nothing for me to do. I scout. I hunt. I can't do those things in this town. It's growing fast, but those aren't talents in high demand."

"Become a surveyor. They always need men to lay out new sections of town."

Fargo barely kept from laughing. The last job in the world he wanted to take was peering through a little tube all day and marking off section of a map so no one else could walk the land. It was the opposite of what he did, how he lived, what he wanted most. Freedom, not constriction.

Again Lydia read his mind.

"When are you going?" she asked.

"I've got a bit more business here," he said, thinking of Rollie King, Hellman, and Schatten. Fargo was not certain how to deal with the politician, but he would, especially since the law had dropped the charges. Letting the man get away with 'Rone's murder rankled worse than a burr under a saddle blanket.

"Schatten?"

"Who else?"

"Let it go, Skye. Gunning him down is no good, even if you owe it to 'Rone." Lydia sat up in bed, distracting Fargo for a moment. She was gloriously naked and hardly noticed

120

the effect she had on him because she was so intent on what she had to say.

"Think about it, Skye, think about all I can offer if you stay." Lydia slipped from the bed and walked lightly to the wardrobe. Fargo watched her every move. Her sleek ivory limbs flashed in the afternoon light slanting through the bedroom window, casting shadows in delightful places, highlighting spots he had explored thoroughly during their lovemaking.

He heaved a deep sigh and climbed from bed. As attractive as the offer was—as attractive as Lydia was—he wanted to be back in the mountains and not rubbing elbows with hundreds of people. Exchanging this freedom for a life with Lydia was mighty tempting, but not tempting enough.

She dressed quickly and so did he. Something gnawed at the edge of his mind, whispering for attention, but he couldn't coax the thought into the full light of day.

"Don't turn your back on Schatten," she said suddenly. "He's got it in for you. If he'd have 'Rone killed, he'll come after you, too."

"I'll keep an eye peeled," Fargo promised. Lydia certainly seemed sure Schatten would try doing his own killing, given the chance. Fargo was not so sure Schatten had ever killed anyone, preferring Lamont and his gang to do the dirty work for him.

"How can I refuse?" he asked, smiling. Lydia came to him and kissed him, but it carried little of the passion she had shown only minutes earlier. In a way, he felt this was a farewell kiss rather than one intended to hold him in her loving web.

Fargo stepped into the hot afternoon sun, squinted, and pulled his floppy-brimmed hat lower to shade his eyes. His Ovaro saw him and neighed excitedly. Fargo knew his horse longed for the freedom of the mountain wilderness, too. He mounted his pinto and rode slowly into town, hunting for Lester Schatten. The politician made himself scarce, and no one, including Marshal Gutherie, knew where he had gone. Fargo held his tongue about King and the deputy's bootlegging to keep from muddying the waters. First Schatten, then the others.

Realizing he could hunt all over Great Salt Lake City for Schatten and not find him without help, Fargo headed back down to the docks to find Old Jess. The merchant had been a gold mine of information before, and Fargo hoped that he would pay out again.

"You ever find that Silas Gentry?" Old Jess asked when Fargo rode up.

"He was right where you said. You must know everything about this town."

"There's nothing worth knowin' that I don't," Old Jess said with some satisfaction. "And the way you asked means you got other things you need to know."

"I can't put anything over on you," Fargo said, laughing. He liked the old man. "Schatten got off scot-free on the murder charges and is avoiding me like the plague."

"That means the law has settled with him but you haven't."

"Something like that," Fargo admitted.

"Marshal Gutherie takes a dim view of folks thinkin' they are better than the law. The judge holds this peculiar view, too."

"I don't plan on staying in Great Salt Lake City much longer."

"It don't pay for a man to be runnin' from a wanted poster. That's no way to spend your life." Old Jess said this as if he knew firsthand. Fargo was curious, but respected the man's privacy. That was the way he wanted to live his life and how he treated others. They dealt fairly with him, and he dealt them the same.

Old Jess sank down to a bench outside his small store, worked a bit on the tobacco plug and then spat a brown gob at the bucket inside the door.

"Well, heard tell that varmint has a place outside town. I don't know where exactly, but him and 'Rone, they—"

"Schatten and 'Rone Clawson?" Fargo interrupted.

"Yep. The two of them was tight for a while. They built this place outside town, but I don't know where. They were partners, or so I've been told." Old Jess spat again. "Then 'Rone took off for some scoutin' over in Wyoming. Don't know if that was what drove 'em apart, but now and then he came back and romanced that lovely little thing." Old Jess stared pointedly at Fargo.

"Lydia Pressman," Fargo supplied.

"She's the one. Quite a looker. Long brunette hair. An

hourglass shape. 'Rone came and went, goin' about his business, romancing her when he blowed through, but Schatten had the inside track, since he was in town all the time and 'Rone wasn't. Then a month or two back 'Rone returned and things changed quick-like. Lydia had eyes only for 'Rone and wanted nothing to do with Lester Schatten after his visit. She even stopped seein' all them other studs that came sniffin' after her. She had quite a following, too."

It didn't surprise Fargo that Lydia had other suitors. He was more interested in what had happened between her, 'Rone and Schatten.

"Why'd she do that?"

"She made her choice. Who can say why a woman picks one man over another?" Again Old Jess fixed him with a hard stare, as if he knew what had gone on between Lydia and Fargo.

Fargo remembered how 'Rone had bragged on Lydia when they teamed up again to scout for Captain Simpson. It was the way a man talked when he had just started a real romance. It was also how a man talked if he knew something he wasn't sharing with his partner.

Fargo came close to putting his finger on the answer, then it slipped away again.

"Want some advice?" asked Old Jess.

"Can I stop you?" Fargo smiled.

"Doubt that's possible," Old Jess said, spitting again. He wiped his mouth on the back of his sleeve. "Forget all about Schatten. He's a snake in the grass and not worth gettin' into trouble over. And forget Lydia Pressman, too. I've seen your ilk enough times to know you don't lasso none too good. She can hold you for a while, but you'll get itchy feet and want to move on."

"I'd feel bad about leaving a woman like her," Fargo said.

"Don't let her hog-tie you. She'll do just fine."

"With Schatten?"

"Who knows? He's not the only mongrel snappin' after her. Never has been." Old Jess spat a final time, stood, and went into the store. "I got work to do. You needin' supplies to get you back on the trail?"

"Not yet," Fargo said. "Soon. Marshal Guthrie told me

they're going to send Carstairs back out to Frémont Island. I want to see him exiled again."

"Flypaper," Old Jess said. "Think on that. I'll see you're outfitted real good. Cheap, too."

Fargo rode back to Lydia's house and spent the night with her, but it wasn't the same. Deep in his heart, he knew it never would be again, no matter how much both of them wanted it to be.

Fargo and Lydia rode together into town, hardly speaking. The distance between them grew, although their legs brushed as Fargo snapped the reins on the horse pulling Lydia's buggy.

"Look there, in the town square," she said, pointing. He brought the buggy to a halt, and they walked a city block to where the crowd gathered.

"What's the occasion?" Fargo asked a deputy trying to keep the crowd from getting unruly. The harried man glanced at him, then answered.

"Marshal Gutherie's getting ready to send that ghoul back to Frémont Island. Nobody figured there'd be this kind of crowd turnin' out to see the son of a buck off." The deputy glanced in Lydia's direction, as if such language might offend her.

"Thanks," Fargo said, pushing through the crowd, making way for Lydia to follow close behind. They got to the front of the throng. He was startled to see the gathering wasn't as peaceable as he had thought. The sharp tang of hot tar made his nose wrinkle and several men hurried forward with pillowcases stuffed with chicken feathers.

"They're going to tar and feather him!" gasped Lydia.

"Looks like it," Fargo said. "It couldn't happen to a worthier individual."

"But that's so cruel," she said.

"Consider what Carstairs did," Fargo replied bitterly. He had been with the man for a spell after saving him from the Crows and had felt a mite sorry for him. But not much. The undertaker was not the kind of man Fargo could absolve of blame for his actions.

"Yes, that's right. He robbed the dead."

"He kept his wife in dead women's clothing, wore jewelry from corpses, and desecrated their graves," Fargo said.

The crowd surged as everyone sought to get a better view. Fargo held Lydia close to keep her from the crush. Together they saw a struggling Carstairs pulled out by Marshal Gutherie and several deputies, Hellman one of them. As Gutherie gave the orders, Deputy Hellman and the others dipped wood paddles in a pitch pot and started smearing the hot tar all over a screaming Carstairs.

"That must hurt," Lydia said.

"Like hell," Fargo answered, then glanced around to see if any in the crowd noticed and objected to his profanity. They were too engrossed in the spectacle of Carstairs being smeared with the hot tar.

A cheer went up when the sacks of feathers were tossed high in the air above Carstairs's head. The white feathers fluttered down like some slow-motion, wind-caught rain. Everywhere a feather touched Carstairs, it stuck. Soon he looked like some writhing, sobbing bird flapping its arms weakly in a vain attempt to take flight.

"Get the smithy!" shouted Gutherie. A man came across the town square lugging a large iron ball. "Get that chained around his leg. Make sure he's not going to slip free of it again."

The loud clanking as a hammer drove in hot rivets to fasten the leg manacle echoed across the square. When the blacksmith finished his work, a tarred-and-feathered Carstairs stood with a new leg shackle and heavy iron ball to keep him from swimming away from Frémont Island.

"He deserves it," Lydia said, but her words were choked, as if she had some sympathy for what the marshal—and the community—did to the grave robber.

"He's not going to get away again!" cried Marshal Gutherie. A cheer went up that showed everyone's approval.

Fargo restrained himself from joining the cheer. Something bothered him, and Marshal Gutherie's words sparked a question.

Carstairs had escaped Frémont Island before, using a leaky boat beached on the far side of the island. This got Fargo thinking again of Rollie King and what he had said to Hellman. King had searched Carstairs for a map. To what? The two bootleggers had expected Carstairs to use the boat they left to get off the island and go straight to—what? Fargo glanced at Lydia as he remembered why King had not been out on the lake to follow Carstairs when he made his escape.

Fargo shook his head. He was turning suspicious of everyone.

"Can you get home all right without me?" Fargo asked suddenly.

"Why, yes, of course. What are you going to do, Skye?" Lydia looked at him, but the question showed only polite interest. He might not have been any more than a casual acquaintance she had happened to meet.

"See Carstairs to the island."

"The marshal or his deputies can do that. You don't think they'll let him go again, do you?"

"No," was all he said. Lydia could get home on her own. He pushed through the crowd and went to the wagon where Gutherie and his men loaded Carstairs into the wagon bed.

"You need someone to escort him out to the island?" Fargo asked.

"Climb in," invited Gutherie. "Reckon you've earned the right to see the varmint back to his exile."

Fargo sank down at the back of the wagon, staring at Carstairs. He wanted to ask the undertaker a dozen questions but held his tongue, since Hellman might overhear. Fargo was increasingly uncomfortable in Great Salt Lake City with all the undercurrents of intrigue flowing around him.

They rode through the streets, a cheering, jeering crowd lining the broad avenues all the way to the dock. Fargo saw young Greenwood had a boat waiting. This time, though, he was alone.

"Which of you gents is going out with the prisoner?" asked Gutherie.

Hellman glanced at Fargo, then shook his head. The rest of the deputies followed his lead.

"I'll be glad to help row him out," Fargo said.

"The job's yours. I paid a dollar before. The rate's the same." Gutherie fumbled out two silver cartwheels and flipped one to Fargo and the other to Greenwood.

"Get him out of our sight," Hellman said, kicking Carstairs as he clumsily got out of the wagon. The undertaker struggled with the heavy iron ball, and the tar and feathers had to be bothering him something fierce. Fargo saw patches of skin that had blistered where hot tar had been applied and had already fallen off, taking flesh with it.

"Into the boat," Greenwood said, making no effort to help Carstairs with the iron ball.

The prisoner sank into the boat, the ball weighing heavily on the bottom.

"Didn't expect to see you again," Greenwood said, looking nervous at what Fargo might say publicly about his hidden vices.

"I'm here to see Carstairs to the island, not make trouble for you. If anything, I wanted to thank you for being so helpful."

Relief flooded the young man. He jerked his head in the direction of the rowboat. "You want me to row?"

"If we both row, that will make the trip go quicker."

Greenwood and Fargo sat side by side, each taking an oar. The deputies shoved them away from the dock, and they began rowing. It took a few strokes for Fargo and Greenwood to coordinate their effort, but when they did the small boat seemed to fly across the lake. As they crossed the distance to Frémont Island, Fargo thought hard on what he wanted to learn from Carstairs.

The undertaker huddled in the prow, moaning to himself and gingerly scraping off what feathers he could. The breeze caught handfuls of white feathers and sent them floating out over the salty waters like miniature clouds. Much of the tar clung tenaciously to his skin, painfully so from all Fargo could see. He and Greenwood put their backs to rowing and before he knew it the boat crunched against the gravelly beach of Frémont Island.

"Out," ordered Greenwood. "This is the last I want to see of you."

"Please," whimpered Carstairs. "Don't leave me like this."

"You want me to shoot you? I don't have a gun." Greenwood glanced at Fargo, seeing his six-shooter strapped to his hip. "Ask him."

"I could have shot him a dozen times over. It's more punishment letting him live," Fargo said.

"Get out," repeated Greenwood.

"I'll get him out," Fargo said, hefting the iron ball for

Carstairs. He sloshed through the salt water lapping against the beach and let the undertaker trail him above the littoral.

"Please, you saved me from those savages. Save me from this cruel punishment!"

"Shut up," Fargo said. He glared at the man, then quelled his anger. "Tell me what Rollie King asked of you the last time you came out here."

Carstairs turned shifty, looking at him from the corner of his eye.

"Will you get me off the island if I tell you?"

"No."

"What's in it for me, then?"

"Maybe it'll go a ways toward evening the score with a lot of people in town," Fargo said. "Maybe your soul will rest a mite easier if you tell."

"He searched me. He said he wanted the map. I don't know what he meant. I never had any map."

"What about the watch?"

"King took it because it was all I had that was worth anything. He kept going on about a map, so I made a deal."

"What kind of deal?" Fargo asked, but he knew the answer from what he had overheard earlier between King and Hellman.

"If he'd get me off the island, I'd give him the map. King told me he'd put a boat on the island later. I—I double-crossed them. I was supposed to meet them at the docks, but I went the other way. I wanted to get away and I don't have any map!"

"Them? King and Hellman?"

"Deputy Hellman?" Carstairs looked startled. He saw he had to say something to enlist Fargo's help. "Hellman might be involved, I don't know. King said he was a member of Lamont's gang," Carstairs stammered out.

"King and Lamont?"

"Lamont and the rest of his gang brought their stolen goods to the far side of the lake. King boasted how he loaded it all into his boat and sold it in Great Salt Lake City. I don't know if he was lying to make himself seem more important or just to scare me."

Fargo considered either a possibility. It made sense that

King was a minor cog in a bigger wheel of crime. He had also seen how King was when he was in his cups.

"When I saw the boat King left, I knew they didn't care anything about me. That leaky boat could have sent me right to the bottom, since I still had the ball and chain on."

"You don't know what the map showed?"

"I never saw any map!" wailed Carstairs. He grabbed at Fargo's arm when he turned to leave. "Help me!"

Fargo could not figure out if he felt more contempt or disgust for the undertaker. He jerked free and went back to where Greenwood waited impatiently to start the return trip—without Carstairs weighing down the boat.

17

"You're bein' mighty quiet, Mr. Fargo," Greenwood said as he rowed beside the Trailsman. "What did that skunk say that disturbed you so much?"

"Nothing that'd concern you," Fargo said, enjoying the physical exertion of pulling the oar. It burned up energy that otherwise would have gone into real worry. Carstairs would lie about anything. The man was a chameleon, changing to fit whatever terrain lay under his worthless belly, but what he had said about King being part of Lamont's gang rang true. That meant Deputy Hellman was in cahoots with Lamont, too, since he called the shots when it came to Rollie King.

What did the map they wanted so badly show, and where was it now? An even uglier speculation began to eat at Fargo. Did Gus Lamont and his gang think 'Rone Clawson had this map? After they had cut 'Rone down, they had stolen his horse. Fargo knew the liveryman had searched the saddlebags but must not have found anything. Otherwise King would not have badgered Carstairs about a map.

Fargo shuddered. If 'Rone had been mixed up with Lamont and his cutthroats, it was possible Schatten had nothing to do with the murder. And if that were true, then Lydia had lied about Schatten bragging to her about it. He had seen Schatten at Lydia's house twice. Lydia had told him Schatten was threatening her, but she had not looked upset until Fargo had inquired after the crooked politician.

Lydia had taken to Fargo in a big way after 'Rone Clawson had been murdered. That much could not be disguised, but an emptiness grew in Fargo's gut when he thought back on all that had happened. Lydia had never come right out and told him to retrieve 'Rone's watch for her, but she had made it mighty plain she would be appreciative.

And she had been. After he had given her the watch, Lydia had grown more distant. All the broken facts swirled and jumbled in his head. He knew the truth. It just didn't fit into a picture he could understand.

"You didn't peach on me and my friends. I appreciate that, Mr. Fargo."

"It must be hard living in such a strict community," Fargo said.

"It's pretty good," Greenwood said. "Sometimes, though, we just get this itch to do . . . wrong."

"Defines what it means to do right," Fargo said, glad that the rowboat had finally returned to the dock. The crowd had drifted away, leaving only a few stalwarts behind to cheer his and Greenwood's return. Marshal Gutherie waited only to see Greenwood nod, then walked off, yelling at the deputies with him to get back to work. He had dispatched a problem and no longer needed to think about Carstairs.

Fargo hoped the undertaker stayed exiled this time. With 'Rone's watch in Lydia's care—and Schatten's?— no one had a reason to help the undertaker escape.

"See you around, Mr. Fargo," called Greenwood. "If you find yourself gettin' a mite thirsty, well, you're welcome to stop by."

"Thank you," he said, but Fargo's thirst was more for truth than liquor at the moment. He hiked back to Lydia's house to get his Ovaro but stopped again at the bottom of the steps. He hesitated to go to her front door knowing what he would find in the small, neatly kept house.

Or what he would not find.

Fargo took all three steps with one long stride and walked to the door. He did not bother knocking as he opened the door and went inside. A quick survey of the house convinced him that she was gone. Her wardrobe was stripped of clothes suitable for the trail. Nowhere did he find 'Rone's watch.

Something about the watch caused all the commotion. Fargo knew he ought to let the matter lie but could not. 'Rone Clawson had been his partner, and he felt he owed the man more than a proper funeral because of the promise he had made as 'Rone lay dying. It was time to complete his obligation by properly looking after Lydia.

Fargo stopped by Old Jess's store and bought what he needed, but when it came to paying, he found he had little more than the dollar Marshal Gutherie had given him to row Carstairs out to Frémont Island.

Old Jess cocked his head to one side and grinned crookedly. "You got eight or nine dollars worth of goods there, Fargo. But that cartwheel, now, that might be worth more to me. Not many merchants in this here town will be able to say they got the money paid for exilin' that son of a bitch undertaker."

"You'd take a dollar for all this?"

"Yes, sir, I will." Old Jess spat accurately at the bucket by the door.

"I hope it brings you a hundred dollars worth of new business," Fargo said appreciatively, flipping the silver dollar to Old Jess. The merchant grabbed it and held it up, letting the sunlight filtering through his dirty store window shine on it.

"If it don't, well then I got me a memento to remember the day I met the Trailsman."

Fargo laughed and shook Old Jess's hand, then gathered his supplies and got on Lydia's trail. Old Jess would be about all he missed in Great Salt Lake City.

Lydia had left her buggy and had taken her horse. Fargo had never seen the woman ride, but thought it would not be hard for her to get a saddle. She might have had one in the small outbuilding behind her house. Fargo circled the house a few times and found fresh tracks leading to the main road.

"Northeast," he said to his Ovaro. As he spoke, he mentally added, *To Camp Floyd.*

Something about the watch and 'Rone Clawson being at Camp Floyd working for the army as a scout fit, but he just could not force the pieces to come together. How did Gus Lamont's gang figure in? Fargo had known 'Rone well enough to know he had not been cut out to be a road agent. Even Rollie King was more of a desperado than 'Rone Clawson could have ever hoped to be.

Fargo rode, occasionally glancing at the road and seeing

nothing but a welter of tracks. He had to take it on faith that Lydia headed for the place where her fiancé had worked last.

Fargo vowed to find out how giving her 'Rone's watch had set her on this trail.

The road curved to the northeast and Wyoming, and Fargo followed it for the rest of the day. Just after sunup the next day, he came to the top of a rise and looked down on a long, sweeping section of road. Far ahead he saw Lydia doggedly riding along, struggling to keep on her horse.

She rode like a man, not sidesaddle, but it was obvious she had little experience as a horsewoman. Fargo smiled, urged his Ovaro down the road, then pursed his lips as he wondered what he ought to do. If he called to Lydia, he might never find out what drew her so powerfully toward Camp Floyd. Trailing her now that he had her in sight would be easy, and by watching he could answer questions that she would never give up voluntarily.

But Fargo got an uneasy feeling as he rode along. Lydia crossed a wide-open expanse and rode into a wooded area beyond. He could not put into words his foreboding until he saw a man emerge from the woods to one side of the road and wave to another a ways off.

Both mounted and rode into the woods, avoiding the road.

Highwaymen!

They had picked Lydia to be their next victim. Fargo knew she would give up more than her money and 'Rone's watch if these men caught her alone in the woods. They would have their way with her and then kill her. He changed his plans and spurred the Ovaro into a gallop. If she spotted him, so be it. He had to stop the two road agents.

Fargo cut off the road and veered into the forest, hot on the tracks of the outlaw who had signaled his partner. It took Fargo a few minutes to realize he was on a well-traveled path that led away from the main road. He glanced to his right, worrying that the outlaws had sized up Lydia as not requiring both of them for the robbery. Before he could change direction and go protect Lydia, the forest opened onto a small clearing. In the middle stood a tumble-down shack.

Fargo had completely misjudged the situation. Or had he? Riding into the clearing from a different direction came Lydia and the other rider. She was in no danger, if the way the man beside her cringed at every hot word meant anything. Fargo could not hear what was being said, but Lydia was in charge.

The rider Fargo had followed walked over and took the reins to Lydia's horse. She started berating both men. Fargo caught snippets of her diatribe then, and knew he had to hear more.

He dismounted and approached the shack from the rear after Lydia and the other two went inside. From here he could spy on them.

"You're letting Gus rot in jail!" Lydia cried. "The judge will hang him and the Kid!"

"Let him look out for himself," one man said sullenly.

"He's your boss. You have to get him out of jail before the trial."

Fargo turned to ice when he heard this. Lydia wanted the men who had backshot her fiancé broken out of jail?

"Where's the rest of the gang?" Lydia asked. "The whole lot of you aren't worth a plugged nickel. Get them and go rescue Gus and the Kid!"

"You're not givin' me orders," one man said. "You kin sleep with Gus, but that don't put you in charge."

"If he gets out and I tell him what you've done—or not done," Lydia threatened. Fargo pressed his eye against the back wall so he could see into the shack. Lydia stood with her balled hands on her flaring hips. One man looked uneasy, but the one she tried to badger into saving Gus Lamont was defiant.

"If Gus don't get out, if he swings, then where's that leave you? Most of us never wanted you around. We didn't care 'bout what you and Gus did, but he's not here now and you're not givin' orders. Right, Eddie?"

The second man's head bobbed furiously. "That's right, Bell."

"You two disgust me."

"Where was you ridin' in such a hurry?" Bell asked. "Never seen you straddlin' a horse before. You always come out in that fancy carriage of yours. Seein' you with your legs spread like that makes me kinda—"

He never got any further. Lydia spit like a mad cat, stepped up and hit him as hard as she could in the belly. Bell doubled over, gasping for air.

"You keep a civil tongue in your head," Lydia snapped. She spun on Eddie, grabbed him by the front of the shirt, and shoved her face into his. "Where's the rest of the gang?"

"O-out waitin' for a stage. Heard tell of a big gold shipment."

She pushed Eddie away and looked at Bell, who still gasped for breath.

"I've got business to tend to."

"You still want us to get Gus out of jail?" asked Eddie.

"Yeah, sure," Lydia said, as if this were far from her thoughts.

Fargo heard Lydia mount and peered around the shack in time to see her ride away, heading back down the trail toward the main road. She had handled the outlaws well— because she was Gus Lamont's girlfriend.

Or was she any man's girlfriend? Fargo considered how she had done everything possible to keep Bell and Eddie from actually going to their leader's rescue. Fargo knew firsthand that Lydia had the charm to convince a man to lasso the moon if need be. Her words had argued for them to save Lamont, but she had said it in such a way to make them rail against her demands. Fargo had to believe she wanted Lamont and the Utah Kid to hang, just as she had wanted him to gun down Schatten.

Lydia was doing all she could to eliminate everyone around her by setting one man against another.

The two in the shack might be members of Lamont's gang, but Fargo had no quarrel with them. It was better to let Captain Simpson take care of the situation. He set out for the edge of the woods to fetch his horse and get back on Lydia's trail when he heard movement behind him.

"You, stop!" Bell shouted the words, but Fargo was already in motion, hand flashing for his gun as he went into a crouch and pivoted around.

Fargo's Colt spat lead a fraction of a second after Bell fired. The outlaw's slug went wide; Fargo's found a bull's-eye in Bell's chest. Fargo dropped to one knee and spun, his six-gun seeking out the other outlaw. Eddie was slower to react, but he had cleared leather.

"Don't!" Fargo warned.

Eddie's eyes darted all over, to his fallen amigo, to Fargo, to his hand holding the gun, then back to Fargo. The outlaw tried to fan his six-shooter. Fargo shot at the same instant Eddie's first slug blasted from the barrel of his pistol.

"You hit me!" cried Eddie, his left arm hanging useless. He cocked his six-shooter and got off a shaky second shot at Fargo.

Fargo had no desire to kill the inept road agent. He aimed carefully and shot a leg out from under Eddie. The outlaw fell facedown and dropped his gun. Fargo cautiously advanced.

"I don't want to kill you. Give up."

"I surrender. Don't kill me like you did Bell!"

Fargo hurried forward when he saw the blood under Eddie expanding rapidly on the sunbaked ground. He kicked away the outlaw's gun, then rolled the man over. Fargo sucked in his breath. His first bullet had broken Eddie's arm. The second might be worse, although Fargo had not intended it that way. He ripped off the road agent's bandanna and whipped it around the man's thigh just above the bullet wound.

"I'm turnin' cold, mister."

"Shut up. I need to put a tourniquet on your leg, or you'll bleed to death." Fargo frantically hunted until he found a short stick to tighten the bandanna. By the time he had it twisted enough to stanch the blood flow, Eddie was pale and trembling.

"Thanks, mister. You ain't such a bad sort, even if you did kill me 'n' Bell."

"Do you ride with Gutherie Lamont?" Fargo had to be sure. Eddie nodded. "What about Lydia Pressman?"

"She's a beauty, ain't she? Always like it when she comes out. Bell wanted her real bad, poor Bell. Thought he could be leader when Gus hangs. . . ." Eddie's words trailed off as he died.

Lamont had used the shack as a rendezvous for his far-flung gang, but only a few mail bags, still stuffed with envelopes, showed any evidence of illegal activities. Fargo rooted around and found a shovel, then went to bury Bell and Eddie.

They should never have thrown down on him.

Fargo rode slowly the remainder of the day, considering what to do about Lydia. He had nothing to show that she had broken any laws. She was a manipulative bitch using men all around her to feather her own nest, but she had not pulled a trigger or stolen a single gold coin. Not that Fargo could prove.

Her skills as a horsewoman improved, and she made better time but still covered far less distance than Fargo would have on his own. He considered circling around her and riding ahead to Camp Floyd, since this was where he believed she was headed, but decided against it. She had shown how unpredictable she could be, and Fargo didn't want to be thrown off the trail by guessing wrong.

Fargo held down his impatience at seeing this through and followed her. He camped without a fire that night and lay staring at the hard, cold stars above. The sounds of the forest and mountains soothed him, and the crisp wind blowing from the higher elevations sang him a lullaby.

"No flypaper stuck to me," he said, remembering Old Tess's warning. Fargo had made the right decision not to stay with Lydia in Great Salt Lake City.

For another day he trailed her, occasionally remembering what it had been like lying next to her warm, sleek, curvy body. Then he forgot those good times and remembered the need for justice that drove him. He had promised 'Rone he would look after Lydia. He would definitely see that she got what she deserved.

For another week he followed her along the narrow road all the way to Camp Floyd. Lydia greeted the sentry cheerily, and then rode straight to Captain Simpson's office. From a ridge a half mile off, Fargo watched and wondered what was going on. Less than twenty minutes later, the captain and Lydia left his office. The captain pointed into the hills, in the direction where 'Rone and Fargo had done their scouting. Then he pointed out other features of the terrain, indicating them on a big map Lydia held.

137

Fargo froze, although he doubted any of them would spot him on the hillside. When the captain went back into his office, Lydia tucked the unwieldy map into her saddlebags, mounted and rode from Camp Floyd, her head held high and haughty.

Fargo rode down to the gate leading into Camp Floyd. The sentry came out, musket at order arms, then recognized him.

"Hey, Fargo, you signin' on for another hitch? We need someone around here who knows what's what."

"Pleased to see you again, Billy," he said, greeting the guard by name. "Can't say I've got it in me for any more mapmaking."

"Dull work, huh?"

"Not as dull as standing guard at the gate," Fargo said, smiling.

"Today's been right busy," Billy said. "You're the second one through. As good as it is to see you again, she was a sight purtier."

"Do tell?"

"Wish the lady'd stayed longer. I reckon Captain Simpson tried to convince her, but she was in a powerful hurry to get somewhere."

"Can I talk to Captain Simpson, or will you shoot me for being an intruder?"

"Go right on up, Fargo. I know he'll be pleased as punch to see you again. The captain's lost two patrols. Might be to the Crows."

Fargo chewed on that as he dismounted in front of the captain's office. Simpson came out, saw who had arrived, and greeted him warmly.

"You're a sight for sore eyes, Fargo. I'm needing—"

"Not this time, Captain. Not for a while. Got some information for you, though."

Simpson peered closely at Fargo.

"Road agents," Fargo supplied. 'They didn't need their mounts anymore." He told the captain where to find the abandoned horses but left out any information about how he had come to shoot the two. "They were riding with Gus Lamont."

"Marshal Gutherie's got him locked up in Great Salt Lake City for murder. Him and the Utah Kid."

"I know that, Captain. I just came from there. These owlhoots are still operating on their own."

Simpson eyed Fargo and then said, "What aren't you telling me? Does it have something to do with the woman who rode through here an hour ago?"

"Why do you say that?" Fargo asked. "About all I know about the remaining gang of Lamont's is that they're after a stagecoach supposed to be carrying a big gold shipment."

Simpson shrugged. "That's not much to go on."

"Reckon not," Fargo said. "This is mighty big country. Might be you can wait for the gang to get back to their hideout. If a few troopers set a trap, you could catch them red-handed."

"Thank you, Fargo," Simpson said. The garrison commander hesitated, then said, "Is there any way I can help you? Whatever it is you're up to with that woman?"

"Things will work out just fine, Captain," Fargo said.

"Come on by in a week or two. There might be a reward waiting for you, if we catch the rest of Lamont's gang. And Fargo?"

"Yes, sir?"

"Keep a sharp eye out."

"Always, Captain, always."

Fargo rode from Camp Floyd, saluted the sentry, who snapped smartly to attention and returned the salute. Then Fargo turned his attention to Lydia's trail. He soon would have every burning question answered one way or the other.

18

Fargo dismounted and advanced on foot, not sure what was happening. He had seen tracks of unshod horses earlier in the day. Definitely Crow ponies. But the band of eight or so Indians had passed by before Lydia had crossed their path, neither spotting the other. Fargo considered the trail for a while and came to the conclusion that the Indians had no idea Lydia was even in the area. It was getting dark and both would be making camp soon.

Fargo perked up when he heard Lydia's voice plainly, but he did not understand what she was saying. She cursed worse than a mountain man, and from the ruckus going up it sounded as if she was having herself a good old-fashioned temper tantrum. He rode to the edge of a small clearing and peered around a lodgepole pine tree sticky with oozing sap.

Lydia had her temper under control now. She trotted to a man standing in the road. From the distance, Fargo could not make out the man's identity, but Lydia was in no danger. Obviously. She slid off her horse and ran to the man, threw her arms around his neck and kissed him the way she had once kissed Fargo.

He felt guilty spying on her, then saw who she kissed so passionately. Lester Schatten.

Fargo tied the reins of his Ovaro to a tree and went closer to spy on the couple. Schatten was even less of a woodsman than Lydia. Fargo had no trouble getting within a dozen feet of Schatten's campfire, where the two huddled together for warmth, as much from each other as from the fire.

"I didn't know if I'd find you," Lydia said. "You said you'd wait for me. When you left town so fast, I worried."

"Why worry? You have it. I don't. And you hightailed it out of town before I did."

"Is the map all you want?" the woman said, piqued. Lydia crossed her arms and stamped her foot at Schatten's lack of tenderness toward her.

"My dear, I've always wanted you, even after you chose 'Rone over me."

"I never chose him over you. Not *that* way, Les."

"All I had was political power. 'Rone had gold, lots of gold."

Fargo hardly believed what Schatten said was true, but Lydia did not deny it.

"I played up to him so we could have it, Les." Lydia snuggled closer to the politician.

"You should have gotten the map before he went to buy the marriage license," Schatten said.

"How was I to know Lamont and the Utah Kid were going to gun him down? If they hadn't killed him, he would have given me the map when he got back. They are such awful, dangerous men. Not like you, Les. You always make me feel so safe."

"I try," Schatten said, bending to kiss her. He pulled away and said, "You ought to give me the map as a wedding present."

"Why get hitched when we can enjoy the honeymoon first?" cooed Lydia.

Fargo listened and wondered what intricate games were being played out. Lydia had insisted that Schatten was responsible for hiring Gus Lamont and his henchmen to kill 'Rone. It sounded to Fargo as if Lamont had gunned down 'Rone to get the mysterious map, and Schatten had nothing to do with it.

The only reason Lydia would have told Fargo that Schatten was boasting of the murder was to incite Fargo to kill him. She seemed pleased enough to be with Schatten now, after her initial outburst of anger at seeing him, but if Fargo had gunned down the politician as revenge for 'Rone's death, Lydia might have been even happier.

She had manipulated Fargo into retrieving the timepiece for her just as she played on Schatten's greed and lust to help her now. Fargo knew the map had to lead to a powerful big treasure.

"I'm glad I found you tonight." The crooked politician put his arm around Lydia's shoulders and pulled her closer. He kissed her again. Fargo watched as their passion grew. He recalled the feeling of Lydia moving under his weight, how she ground against him and responded physically, crying out in unbridled desire as they made love. Now she was doing all that for Lester Schatten.

He slipped back into the forest, returned to his horse and a cold, tasteless meal and an even colder bed.

Fargo crept toward Lydia and Schatten's campsite just before sunup, intending to take them both back to Camp Floyd and let Captain Simpson sort out their tangled crimes. He ducked back fast when a rock came his way. Another quick peek around a tree convinced him she had not spotted him. The rock had been thrown in a different direction. In her anger she had missed by a country mile and just happened to almost brain him.

"How could you, you miserable cur! You son of a bitch! You . . . you monster!" The woman ranted some more, storming about the small area. Then she started kicking at rocks and logs. As she moved she stirred up a small dust cloud. Fargo couldn't make head nor tail of it.

Then it hit him. Schatten was nowhere to be seen.

He let Lydia continue her tirade for several more minutes until she was tuckered out. The lovely woman sank to a rock, put her face in her hands and wept. Only then did Fargo venture out. As he advanced, he looked all around. He did not suspect a trap, but these were dangerous woods. The Crow party was on its way somewhere, and Lydia had shown she was not to be trusted.

Other unseen dangers ran through his mind, but Lester Schatten remained right on top. Schatten was a backshooter and might be setting a trap, if he had gotten wind of Fargo on his trail.

Fargo rested his hand on the Colt hanging at his hip, then stopped and waited for Lydia to notice him. It took a minute more. She sniffed loudly, wiped her nose on the back of her sleeve, and stood. When she saw him she let out a yelp of panic.

"Skye! What are you doing here? I didn't expect to see you again."

"Looking for Schatten?" he asked. "Or did he rob you and then desert you?"

Fargo looked around the camp and saw only Lydia's bedroll. No supplies remained, and only her horse nervously cropped at the succulent grasses at the edge of the clearing.

"How'd you know about him?" Lydia clamped her mouth shut, swallowed, then composed herself. "I should have known you would figure it out. It surprised me 'Rone hadn't told you."

"We were partners, but 'Rone had a way of keeping to himself. That didn't bother me much."

"That's the way you are, too," Lydia said. She sniffed again and finally got her rampaging emotions under control. "I know."

"How are you and Schatten hooked up together?" Fargo wasn't sure he wanted to hear the sordid story.

"You mean, how did the man responsible for killing my fiancé and I come to be out here in Wyoming together? Or—"

"Don't lie," Fargo said sharply. "Gus Lamont killed 'Rone, not Schatten."

"He paid for it! He—" Lydia stopped her protests when she saw Fargo's expression. "Skye darling, you don't know what 'Rone was mixed up in. He was part of Lamont's gang and did terrible things."

"No, he didn't," Fargo said, increasingly disgusted with her lies. A thought occurred to him. "You were with Rollie King when Carstairs escaped from Frémont Island, weren't you? You thought he had taken the map off Carstairs earlier. That's why Carstairs got away."

"King was such a fool," Lydia said angrily. "He had the map and never knew it. By the time I got to him, he had lost it. None of that matters, Skye. We're together now. We can get the map."

"Do you want me to kill Schatten?" Fargo asked.

"Of course! What difference does it make if he didn't pay Lamont to gun down 'Rone? He's mixed up in this up to his ears. King and Hellman brought all that Lamont stole into town to fence. Who do you think bought supplies for Lamont? Schatten did, after he took his cut!"

"How do you know this?" Fargo saw a different woman now. This Lydia Pressman had her hand in anything that might make her a dollar, and she used all the men to do it. Fargo didn't want to think how she had expertly maneuvered him into hunting for 'Rone's watch, but she had. He actually thought he was doing her a favor, that giving her the watch was something 'Rone had wanted.

Fargo smiled grimly, knowing Lydia would lie about her connection with Gus Lamont. But what if she didn't? What would he do if she fessed up and threw herself on his mercy? He had no proof she had done anything illegal, even if she had surrounded herself with outlaws.

"I didn't want any part of this. I . . . just got mixed up with Schatten because I thought he was a decent man. When I found out he worked for Lamont, I knew different, but it was too late. Will you help me, Skye? We were so good together. We can be again. You were the only one who ever meant anything to me."

"Are you mixed up with Lamont?"

"Of course not!" she cried. "What ever gave you that idea?"

"What about the watch?" he asked, holding his anger in check. She had solved a problem for him by denying she was involved with Gus Lamont.

She gritted her teeth and looked ready to chew nails and spit tacks. "He took it, the scoundrel!" Lydia said, finally settling down a little. "The really important thing is the map Captain Simpson gave me. I'm lost out here without it. But you know the terrain, don't you?"

There was something more she wasn't telling him, but Fargo was at a loss to figure out what it was. She was mad at Schatten, but not stricken that he would find whatever treasure 'Rone had left behind. Lydia still tried to get him to do her dirty work for her by inciting him to kill Schatten.

" 'Rone and I rode every last inch of it together," Fargo said.

"I could have died. He took all my food, every bit of supplies. He even stole my saddlebags! Lester Schatten's a killer, Skye. He wanted me dead!"

" 'Rone found where Lamont's gang hid their loot. He moved it and put a map into the watchcase. Is that what the map shows?" Fargo remembered the deep scratches inside the case. He had ignored them and wished he had paid more attention.

"You're right, Skye. Help me find what 'Rone left as his legacy and we . . . we can share it." Lydia moved closer. Her warm hand rested on his arm. "That's not all you can have, either."

He said nothing, staring at her with new eyes. She would say and do anything. Had he missed this selfishness before, or just gotten caught up in 'Rone's murder? Lydia was a good actress and even better in bed, but that was no excuse for him being so blind.

"Go after him, Skye. Get the watch back. Do it for 'Rone. Do it for yourself. Do it for me." Lydia's voice dropped to a husky, sexy whisper. She kissed him, but Fargo's heart was not in it. She backed off and looked at him as if she had not noticed his lack of enthusiasm. In the same low voice she said, "Get the watch back, and there'll be plenty more where that came from."

"I'm sure there will be," he said, irony in his words. Lydia missed the tone entirely.

"When can you get on his trail?" she asked.

"Right now," Fargo said. "Get saddled. You're coming with me." A thousand thoughts raced through his mind. The Crows hunted in the area, what remained of Lamont's gang intended to rob a stage—and there was Schatten. Fargo could not figure out where Schatten really fit in, what with all of Lydia's lies and the way it looked that the politician had plotted to kill 'Rone Clawson.

Most of all, Fargo wanted to keep an eye on Lydia.

As they set out, Fargo decided speed was Schatten's ally. He rode flat out and devil take the hindmost. Then again, as far as the Great Salt Lake City politician knew, Lydia was the only one likely to be after him.

Fargo chose a steady pace rather than hurrying along because the trail was plain and he didn't want to tire the Ovaro. When he found Schatten, he wanted to be fresh for the fight. And a fight it would be, too. The man had a great deal to answer for, if even a fraction of what Lydia rattled on about was true.

The way got rockier, and Fargo found himself spending more time hunting for the trail. Schatten never deviated from a straight path down into a long valley that led to the Overland Pass Fargo and 'Rone had so recently mapped.

It had been along the road in that pass where much of the thieving had gone on, probably by Lamont's gang.

"Oh, Skye," sighed Lydia. "This is so beautiful. I can see why you love it out here so much, you and 'Rone. What a wonderful place for us to be together."

Fargo surveyed the broad green valley with a winding river tumbling over slick rocks down the middle. The valley joined the pass through the mountains not five miles off to the east. This was lush land, good for grazing cattle or sheep, maybe for raising crops as well. Fargo closed his eyes and tried not to think of the settlers pouring into the land, running it over. He wanted to remember it this way, wild and free and open to any man with the sand to explore it.

Fences and herds and towns would only ravage such fine untamed, wide-open territory.

Worst of all, he had done his part scouting and mapping for Captain Simpson to make certain the land would be opened to settlers.

"There!" cried Lydia. "There's the son of a bitch!" She pointed into the valley. At first Fargo did not see him. Fargo finally spotted Schatten on foot near the river. He tried to make out what the man was doing but couldn't. Schatten turned in circles, then threw up his hands as if in exasperation. Then the politician dropped to one knee and began the strange ritual all over again.

"Stay here," he told Lydia. "I'll capture him."

"Kill him, Skye. It's the safest way. He's a murdering swine. Shoot him down before he can kill again."

Fargo glared at her until she subsided. Contritely, Lydia said, "I'm sorry. It's just that he's done so many terrible things to both of us. Do what you think is best, Skye. Be careful and keep your eye on him."

She would have kissed him if he had let her. Fargo turned his Ovaro away, hunting for the best path down into the valley, where Schatten still performed his pointless ritual of turning and crouching, spinning and pointing.

As he made his way into the valley, Fargo checked his weapons. The Henry rode easy in the saddle sheath. It might be worth his while to get within range and take out Schatten that way. Even as the thought crossed his mind, Fargo discarded the notion, since it was what Lydia wanted.

Schatten might be a lowdown no-account coyote, but Fargo was better than that. He wanted to see the expression on Schatten's face when they met and the politician realized he was caught and going back to Great Salt Lake City to stand trial.

Fargo never knew what gave him away. Schatten was hunting for some landmark, some distinctive outcropping of rock or tall tree marked by 'Rone on his map and could not find it. During that search the politician must have spotted Fargo making his way down the side of the valley. The first bullet missed Fargo's head by a mile.

The second almost took it off.

His hat went spinning through the air, forcing him to duck low. He urged his horse ahead. Fargo hunted for cover but had reached a spot where nothing seemed safe enough. A third bullet made him cringe as it left a bloody, shallow nick on his shoulder.

He finally reached a tumble of rocks and hit the ground running. The Ovaro reared and trotted off, but Fargo knew it wouldn't go far. He could whistle and the horse would come back after he caught Schatten.

"Why are you so all-fired intent on coming after me, Fargo?" shouted the politician. Fargo knew better than to poke his head up. Schatten would shoot it off. "Lamont killed your partner, not me. Gus and the Utah Kid are standing trial for their crime. I had nothing to do with the shooting—or them."

"That's not the way Lydia tells it," Fargo called.

"Lydia!" Schatten spat the name as if it burned his tongue. "She's double-crossed everyone, Fargo. Don't let her dupe you, too. She's downright evil!"

Fargo knew Schatten was on the move, trying to get a clear shot. If he stayed put, he would eventually wind up in the man's rifle sights. He looked around and saw the spot to make his attack. Fargo took a deep breath, then ran for all he was worth.

Bolting like a frightened rabbit took Schatten by surprise. The man's first shot missed Fargo by a wide margin. Fargo reached Schatten before the man got off a second.

Head down and charging like a bull, Fargo smashed his shoulder into Schatten's midriff. The man grunted, stumbled, and fell with Fargo on top of him. Fargo jerked the rifle from the politician's hands.

"I give up," Schatten gasped out. "You got me, Fargo."

"Get to your feet," Fargo said. He had wanted Schatten to put up more of a fight so he could have the satisfaction of punching him repeatedly.

"What are you going to do now?" asked Schatten. "The map in the watch is no good, unless you know the key. A tree or rock or something. I couldn't figure out what it was when I—"

The gunshot startled Fargo. He stared at Schatten as the man sank to the ground like a marionette with its strings cut.

The sound of a light footstep behind him wasn't enough warning. A heavy blow knocked him to his hands and knees, momentarily stunning him. A second, harder blow knocked him unconscious.

19

Half his face was warm. The other half was cold. Fargo stirred, then sank back to the ground, moaning. Bees buzzed loudly in his ears and his head felt as if it had turned rotten like a melon and fallen apart. When he blinked and got dirt in his eyes, he jerked back and put together all the tiny details.

He had been lying with his face against the cold soil while the hot summer sun boiled the other part of his face. And the pain in his skull caused him to wince with the smallest movement. Slowly, the pain receded and Fargo was able to think more coherently.

"Lydia," he said, knowing who had slugged him without studying the tracks behind in the dirt. He stumbled to Schatten's body and found that both the survey map and 'Rone's watch were gone. Looking around caused Fargo some more pain in his head, and the world spun in weird, wild waves. He waited for the sensation to ebb and then stood unsteadily.

Not only were the map and watch gone, so were Schatten's horse and the supplies he had stolen from Lydia. He rubbed the lump on his head, and his fingers came away bloody. Walking slowly, he made his way to the river and used his bandanna to wash the wound. After he had done what he could to patch himself up, he sat on the riverbank and dipped his bandanna in the water again, washing his face and trying to keep his temper.

Fargo found himself as mad at himself as he was at Lydia for her treachery. He should have been more careful dealing with her. He had figured out she was about the most dangerous of all the people he dealt with, and that might include Gus Lamont.

"She was in too big a hurry to do the job right," Fargo

said aloud. The echoing words in his skull caused more pain, but it faded away slowly like a bad memory. Lydia should have killed him if she didn't want him on her trail. Just taking Schatten's horse as she had wouldn't slow Fargo one bit.

Rather than get on the woman's trail, Fargo had a disagreeable chore to do. Fargo thought on leaving the man where he had died but concluded even a crooked politician deserved a better end than being eaten by buzzards. He dragged Schatten's body to softer ground, then began digging a grave. Not much, not deep, but enough to put a thin layer of dirt over the body so he could stack the grave with rocks to keep the coyotes from digging up the corpse.

He considered putting a crude cross to mark the grave, then decided against it.

"Burn in hell." Fargo's words blanketed the grave as the final layer between Schatten and the living world. If there was any forgiveness for Lester Schatten's sins, it wouldn't come from the Trailsman.

Brushing off his hands, Fargo walked from the grave and went to the spot where he had seen Schatten struggling to find landmarks. He turned slowly, studying every point of the compass. 'Rone had liked this area, commenting on its wild beauty when the two of them had mapped it. Fargo imagined his partner mentioning this spot to Lydia, telling her how they could settle here, even boasting of the striking scenery.

Fargo stared at a distant peak. The soaring crag was easily the most prominent feature in sight, dominating the peaceful valley. If 'Rone had wanted to pick a landmark, he could not have chosen a better one.

Fargo walked past Schatten's grave and then toward the woods where he had left his Ovaro. Not seeing the horse didn't bother him. Fargo put his fingers in his mouth and whistled loudly. He listened for a reply, but heard nothing. A second whistle brought the pinto trotting out of a lightly forested area where the grazing might have been better. He patted the horse's muzzle, then fished through his saddlebags and found a lump of sugar to feed to the Ovaro.

He felt a little better and would be in improved spirits once he found Lydia.

'Rone Clawson had not lived high, wide, and fancy free

but what scout could on the paltry sum the U.S. Army paid? Before he and Fargo had taken the mapping chore, they had come and gone their separate ways a few times in the prior year. Fargo had never seen any evidence of 'Rone having more money than he could explain.

Fargo snorted. He had never seen 'Rone with *any* money. 'Rone and money had been strangers more often than friends. That made for a powerful lot of temptation, if 'Rone had found where Lamont's gang stashed their loot.

Riding slowly, he eventually found Lydia's tracks. She was even worse than Schatten about leaving a trail. Two horses, on soft ground, past bushes with branches that snapped easily, across the river and out directly on the other side—it was almost too easy.

He began worrying she was leading him into an ambush, then Fargo discarded such a notion as ridiculous. She could have killed him when he was out cold. For all he knew, Lydia had thought she had slain him. The second blow would have cracked a lesser man's skull wide-open and spilled his brains.

The sun set sooner than Fargo would have liked, but he knew he had been unconscious the better part of the day. He made camp and ate some jerky, thinking about what he would do to Lydia when he found her as he chewed the tough, dry, salty meat. 'Rone's treasure had to exert a powerful, greedy pull on her, or she would have offered to share it sooner. As that thought came to him, Fargo remembered Lydia saying in passing she wanted him to stay in Great Salt Lake City. Had she been shining him on or had she been serious then?

He shook his head. Flypaper, Old Jess had said. Fargo had to shake off the last trace of that flypaper or it would stick to him forever.

Fargo found a spot to make camp for the night, curled up in his blanket and slept. He awoke just before dawn, his head throbbing like a rotted tooth. The way his vision doubled and then cleared worried him a mite. Blows to the head sometimes did this to a man, and Fargo did not want Lydia's curvaceous image going double if he had to defend himself.

It would be a waste to fire two bullets, one at each image, if he could get by with only a single round.

As the sun poked above the pass and sent bright rays glinting off the ribbon of river there, he was on the trail again. Lydia's path had taken on a single-minded determination to go straight to the base of the crag he had noted from where Schatten had died.

Fargo shaded his eyes with his hand and scanned the rim of the valley. The only distinctive rock formation in sight was still the sharp, rocky needle—and it was right in line with Lydia's trail. A greenhorn would follow the map exactly, not daring to deviate from the course laid out.

Rather than continue after her, he scouted a bit and found a winding trail a mile off that led to the valley rim. Taking it proved a longer, but easier path to the top. As he neared the rock needle, he heard Lydia cursing and struggling with her and Schatten's horses just over the edge and a dozen yards below him along a narrow trail.

Fargo backed off, found a secluded area to tether his Ovaro, and then went to see what she did once she reached the summit near the distinctive rock spire.

He had just settled down in the shade of a windswept blue spruce tree when the woman tumbled over the edge of the valley rim and almost dragged the two horses with her. She wiped sweat from her forehead and had a wild look in her eye, as if she would explode at any instant.

From his vantage point, Fargo saw her spread out the map and carefully position the watch so its opened lid was properly aligned. In spite of everything, Fargo still found her seductively enchanting. This wild look became Lydia Pressman. She seemed more a creature of the forest and hills than a city dweller, and being in her proper element enhanced her natural beauty. Her brown hair floated in disarray around her face like a delightful, delicate cloud. Breasts rising and falling heavily as she became more excited in her hunt, she hiked her skirts to show her trim ankles as she hurried away toward the rock spire.

Fargo remembered those long, sleek legs well. And her breasts. Not to mention the way her ruby lips had touched him here and there, just in the right ways. He remembered it all, and it no longer meant a damned thing to him. She had ambushed him and murdered Schatten. That made her no better than her lover, Gus Lamont.

Making certain his six-shooter rode easy on his hip,

Fargo followed her. She had dropped the reins of the horses and had hurried on ahead. Fargo was ready to whip his weight in wildcats.

From the way Lydia acted, he might just have to do that.

Walking as if on eggshells, he followed her to the rock column and saw she had gone down a stony path to a small cave ten feet below. He heard a triumphant shout, followed by the clumsy sounds of Lydia's search for 'Rone's treasure. The triumph turned to cries of utter desolation. Fargo was warned in time to fade back and find a crevice large enough to hide as she came out.

The set of her shoulders would have been enough to tell him she had not found what she expected in the cave. The expression on her face was one of utter devastation. She went to the edge of the path and looked down into the peaceful valley. Fargo started to pry himself free of the crevice to walk over to her when it seemed she would throw herself over the edge to her death.

Lydia sagged, defeated, but did not jump. She cried a while, then held up 'Rone Clawson's watch and heaved it out into space with all her strength. It turned over and over in the bright summer sun, then disappeared to smash into the rocks below. This act of defiance seemed to ease Lydia's anger and sorrow, and she edged back from the brink. Her dusty cheeks were streaked with rivers of tears. She wiped at her nose with the back of her hand as she passed within a few feet of where he hid, never guessing anyone was nearby. Fargo could tell she fought to keep from a new wave of weeping. She stumbled to the top of the trail, grabbed at the reins of the horses, and started back down into the valley. She was so distraught that she never noticed Fargo and even left behind Schatten's horse.

Fargo squeezed out of the rock crevice and went to the edge, watching as Lydia made her way back down the treacherous trail. It had never occurred to her that an easier trail, such as the one Fargo had found, might exist. He saw her vanish around a hairpin turn and eventually did not even hear her on the trail any longer.

Curious at what she had found, Fargo ducked and went into the small cave. It broadened and the roof angled up so Fargo could stand straight. The light sneaking into the cave showed rows of wooden boxes. He saw Lydia had broken several open, spilling the contents on the dusty cave floor.

Bags of beans, a case of brand new Spencer rifles, ammunition, stacks of airtights of peaches and tomatoes, even piles of wool blankets had been cached here. This was truly a treasure, should a man have need of survival gear. But Lydia had obviously thought there would be something more and had not found it.

Fargo sat on the case of rifles, wondering where everything in the cave had come from. Possibly this was the booty taken by Lamont's gang, but it hardly seemed worth the effort if 'Rone had found it somewhere else and moved it. Some things were more precious than gold on the frontier. Things like rifles, ammunition, and food.

But not to outlaws like Gus Lamont.

Fargo started to leave, then sat back down to think. Why would 'Rone even mention the cave to Lydia, much less scratch a map inside his watch? And why wouldn't he have said something to his partner while they were in the area and could have used the food and blankets? Captain Simpson would have ponied up a nice reward for the rifles and ammunition. 'Rone had known how difficult it was for the commander at Camp Floyd to get decent supplies. It didn't make sense that he would have kept this kind of "treasure" a secret from everyone but his fiancée.

"He would have told me if all he'd found was supplies," Fargo said, thinking aloud. "And he would have wanted gold to win Lydia away from Schatten."

Fargo began a more careful search of the cave, finding what he expected at the rear of the cave. Slats from a crate had been laid over a narrow shaft, then covered with rock and dust to camouflage it. Fargo pushed it aside and peered down into total blackness.

He had not found any miner's candles in the cave. If he made a torch and lit it, he might choke to death from the smoke in the tight passage. He wasn't thrilled with the idea, but knew he had to go down without any light. Screwing up his courage, Fargo wiggled down the tight passage, his shoulders hunched so he could fit into the rock chimney. For a frightening moment, he feared the shaft went to the center of the earth. He slipped down inch by inch until his boots finally touched solid rock. By twisting and turning, he scrambled onto hands and knees in the pitch-black space beneath the cave.

Groping about he found a leather bag. Hefting it made him smile. Fargo spent the next hour blindly exploring the small chamber and piling over a dozen leather bags where he could get them up the shaft and into the upper cave.

When he got the bags where he could open them and look inside, his heart raced.

Gold dust. Silver coins. A small fortune *had* been stashed in the cave. 'Rone's dowry to marry the most beautiful woman in all Great Salt Lake City. His way of convincing Lydia to marry him rather than Lester Schatten. When 'Rone had discovered the cave was something Fargo could not figure, but what he knew of 'Rone's character told him the man had discovered the outlaws' hidden loot rather than stealing the bounty himself. This was where a good man had turned dishonest because of a woman's love.

'Rone had seen in the loot a way to win and keep Lydia, although none of it was his to keep.

Fargo lugged the bags out and stuffed them into his saddlebags, then into those on Schatten's horse. The animals shied under the considerable weight, but he wouldn't slow down. He had to catch Lydia and take her along with the loot to Captain Simpson. When she was safely locked up in the Camp Floyd stockade, Fargo could pass along the location of this cave. Simpson could use the rifles and other supplies inside, and then get down to trying Lydia for her crimes. Everyone at Camp Floyd would learn what type of woman she really was. Once she was convicted, Fargo would see that her misdeeds were made public in Great Salt Lake City. 'Rone had asked him to "See to Lydia," and Fargo was nothing less than a man of his word.

Old Jess had been right. Anything as sticky as flypaper was bound to cause trouble. 'Rone had not been strong enough to pull free, but Fargo was. He would see that it was tossed aside so no one else would get tangled up. Then he would move on. The trail ahead stretched to the horizon and freedom, and no man alive was better at following that trail than The Trailsman.

LOOKING FORWARD!

**The following is the opening
section from the next novel in the exciting
Trailsman series from Signet:**

THE TRAILSMAN #232
PACIFIC PHANTOMS

---

*Oregon, 1861—When deadly spirits haunt a mining
town, it's up to the Trailsman to put them to
rest . . . permanently.*

The big man in buckskins had no idea he was being
watched as he reined up beside a swift mountain stream.
Swinging lithely down from his pinto stallion, he stretched,
flexing his broad shoulders. He had been on the trail for
days and his muscles were stiff from riding. As his piercing
lake-blue eyes roved over the stately ranks of Douglas fir
that covered a nearby slope, a jay squawked at him from
its roost high up on a branch. Elsewhere in the shadowed
depths of the woods a squirrel chattered.

Skye Fargo smiled as he sank onto a knee and removed
his hat. The western half of the new state of Oregon was a
lush wilderness largely unexplored by whites. Just the sort of
verdant paradise he liked most, where a man could lose himself for days and weeks on end, living off the land and gener-
ally doing as he pleased without anyone to tell him different.

Bending, Fargo dipped his hand into the cold, clear water
and cupped some to his mouth. It tasted delicious.

He was traveling west over the Cascade Mountains and in

another day or so would reach the Willamette Valley, his destination. In his back pocket was the letter that had brought him. That, and the promise of five thousand dollars. At the moment he was practically broke and badly needed the money.

Dipping his hand into the stream again, Fargo froze at the distinct metallic rasp of a rifle lever. Someone had come up behind him, his stealthy tread drowned out by the gurgling water. If this stranger had intended to kill him, Skye reasoned, he could have done so from ambush, so evidently he wanted Skye alive. For the moment, at least.

"Don't move, mister," a gruff voice demanded. "We don't aim to harm you, but me and the boys will put windows in your skull if you make a play for that six-shooter on your hip."

Now Fargo knew there was more than one. He sensed rather than heard someone idle up close enough to snatch his Colt and step back again.

"Stand up and turn around," the spokesman ordered. "Nice and slow, if you please. You can put your hat on but keep your hands where we can see 'em."

Fargo did as he was told. Four men had guns trained on him. The apparent leader was a big-boned character in homespun clothes and scuffed black boots, the Colt now wedged under his wide brown leather belt. Beside him stood a lean fellow with a nose as long as a buzzard's beak and an Adam's apple the size of a horseshoe. The third man was a grizzled oldster whose faded buckskins had seen much better days. The fourth, to Fargo's mild surprise, was an Indian, a short, stocky mass of muscle in a high-crowned black hat, dusky shirt, and brown shirt, his raven hair cropped just below the ears.

A Modoc, Fargo guessed. It was rare to encounter them so far north.

"Who might you be, friend?" the leader asked. "And what in hell are you doing in this neck of the woods?"

"I don't see where it's any business of yours," Fargo responded good-naturedly enough. They didn't strike him as being run-of-the-mill cutthroats. He assumed they had an excuse for what they were doing and he was willing to hear them out so long as they didn't start anything.

"That's where you're wrong." The man in homespun encompassed the surrounding mountains with a sweep of his arm. "This land belongs to Luther Brunsdale. Maybe you've heard of him? He's one of the richest, most powerful gents in all of Oregon. And he don't cotton to folks traipsing over his property as they see fit."

"He owns all this?" Fargo was impressed. There had been nothing in the letter to indicate how vast Brunsdale's holdings were.

"And lots more, besides. Some say he has the biggest stretch of prime timberland between the Columbia River and Sacramento."

"Lucky him," Fargo said dryly.

"Luck had nothing to do with it. Mr. Brunsdale laid claim to all this country pretty near twenty years ago. He's worked hard to make the Brunsdale Timber Syndicate what it is today. The newspapers call him a timber baron and say he's carved out a regular empire."

"You work for him, I take it?"

"We all do. I'm Tom Poteet. Ordinarily I work as a flume herder, but Mr. Brunsdale has a lot of us out beatin' the brush, huntin' the vermin who murdered over a dozen people so far."

The older man in buckskins gestured. "Quit your jawing, Tom. How do we know this coon ain't in cahoots with them? I say we take him down to the line camp. Dinsmore will know what to do."

"I reckon you're right, Grizwald," Tom Poteet said.

The skinny man had been admiring the Ovaro the whole time, and now he moved toward it, saying, "I claim the horse. My feet are plumb wore out from all this hiking around." He reached for the reins.

"No!" Fargo said, taking a step.

Instantly, the four men tensed, Grizwald training a Sharps on his sternum, the Modoc taking a bead squarely on his forehead.

"I beg your pardon?" the stringbean said, seeming amused.

"No one rides my animal but me," Fargo stated. It was the principle of the thing. On the frontier a man's horse was as much a part of him as his clothes, and it was unthinkable for anyone to use another's mount without permission.

"Is that a fact?" Smirking, the skinny man grabbed the reins anyway.

"I won't tell you twice," Fargo warned.

Tom Poteet turned to the smug troublemaker. "Maybe it's best if you don't, Oddie. No sense in givin' this gent a hard time until we know who he is and what he's doing in these parts."

"I told you," Oddie said, moving next to the saddle, "I'm tuckered out. I'm a bucker, not a damned bull whacker. I'm not used to all this walking. It won't hurt if I ride down to the line camp." He grabbed the saddle horn and lifted a boot to the stirrup.

Fargo tensed, waiting for the explosion sure to follow. The stallion didn't take to being ridden by strangers, as Oddie learned a heartbeat later when the pinto nickered and reared, knocking Oddie backward.

"Damn you!" Compounding his stupidity, Oddie held on to the reins, which incited the Ovaro into prancing to one side to pull free. In doing so, the stallion stepped in front of Grizwald and the Modoc.

It was the opening Fargo needed. A long bound brought him to Tom Poteet and he drove his right fist into Poteet's gut. He regretted slugging the man, but he had the Ovaro to think of. As Poteet buckled, Skye yanked on the Colt, pivoted, and slammed the barrel against the side of Oddie's head with enough force to crumple Oddie where he stood. Another bound, and he was astride the pinto and cutting sharply on the reins.

Grizwald had lowered his Sharps and started to run around in front of the stallion. Caught flat-footed, he was battered aside, lost his balance, and fell.

That left the Modoc, who moved in closer and elevated his rifle. A flick of Fargo's leg swatted the barrel aside just as the man squeezed the trigger. The slug meant for him whizzed harmlessly into the forest canopy, and before the Modoc could fire again, Fargo was across the narrow stream and in among the douglas firs, riding hell-bent for leather while bent low over the saddle.

"Stop him!" Poteet yelled.

Excerpt from PACIFIC PHANTOMS

A rifle boomed, but Fargo had veered to the left and the bullet clipped a branch a yard away. Within moments he was out of their sight, and safe, bearing westward. He heard Oddie and Grizwald cussing up a storm, their outbursts rapidly fading as he held to a gallop for the next quarter of a mile.

Convinced no one was after him, Fargo slowed to a walk and assessed the situation. He saw no reason to change his plans. Now that he had an inkling of why he was needed, it was more important than ever he find the man who had sent for him.

The blazing afternoon sun was warm on Fargo's face as he descended a wooded slope to a grassy shelf that afforded a sweeping vista of the foothills below, and gave him his first glimpse of the Willamette Valley miles beyond. For decades now, the fertile valley had lured Easterners by the thousands with its promise of prime farmland for the taking. To them, Oregon was the Promised Land, and they were more than willing to endure the severe hardships of the Oregon Trail in order to see that promise fulfilled.

About two miles to the northwest smoke from a campfire curled skyward. The line camp, Fargo guessed, and rode on down over the rim toward it. The letter had not been all that specific about how to reach Brunsdale's, the men at the line camp were bound to know.

The first were replaced by madrones, ash, and pines. Thick undergrowth limited the range of Fargo's vision, and he rode with his hand on the butt of his Colt. After what the four men had told him, he had to be ready for anything.

In a quarter of a mile the vegetation thinned at the border of a high-country meadow sprinkled with bright yellow flowers. Butterflies flitted breezily about, and several doe grazed along the tree line.

Drawing rein, Fargo scanned the meadow carefully. It wouldn't do to venture into the open until he was sure he wouldn't be ambushed. He was about to tap his spurs against the stallion when movement at the far end of the meadow alerted him to a rider approaching from across the way. Possibly another of Brunsdale's men, he thought, until the rider emerged from deep shadow into the brilliant light of day.

It was a woman, a tall blonde whose golden locks cascaded over her shoulders in luxurious curls. She had high, full cheekbones, an oval chin, and red lips as full and inviting as ripe cherries. Only in her early twenties, she had on a green riding outfit complete with a matching wide-brimmed hat, and was mounted on a magnificent Palomino with a flowing mane and tail. Her saddle was the best money could buy, a fancy affair studded with enough silver to make a *vaquero* drool with envy.

Intrigued by the woman's beauty, Fargo was content to let her cross toward him rather than risk scaring her off by showing himself.

Humming to herself, the blonde was idly gazing down at the yellow flowers, not at the forest where she should. She was about midway when a hint of motion above her drew Fargo's gaze to a glittering shaft streaking out of the air.

"Look out!" Fargo bawled, whipping his reins and hurtling from the trees.

Startled, the blonde glanced up just as the arrow struck her saddle. Narrowly missing her thigh, it imbedded itself in the pommel, causing the Palomino to rear. Although the woman clutched at the horn, she was pitched backward and fell, landing on her back in the high grass. She leaped right back up but her mount was fleeing to the south.

Another arrow arced out of the blue, thudding into the ground an arm's length from where she stood.

"Get down!" Fargo shouted, but the blonde did no such thing. She saw him rushing toward her and in her confusion she apparently assumed he was somehow to blame for her plight. She whirled and ran—away from him, toward the very spot where the arrows were coming from.

"No! I'm trying to help!" Fargo yelled, but he was wasting his breath. The woman was making for the trees with the speed of an antelope, her tanned face twisted toward him.

Off in the forest a shadowy shape materialized.

"Watch out! In front of you!" Fargo roared, pointing.

Finally, the blonde heeded him and faced the wall of vegetation just as another shaft was loosed. The arrow flashed toward her heart like a bolt of wooden lightning. Fargo thought for sure she was a goner. But almost at the last split-second she hurled herself forward onto her stomach, her hat flying off as she dived, and the shaft pierced her hat instead of her body.

Palming the Colt, Fargo banged off two swift shots at the archer. Whoever it was melted into the greenery, and before another arrow could be fired, Fargo reined to a halt beside the winsome beauty and extended his hand. "Hurry! Up behind me!"

To her credit the woman didn't argue. Springing erect, she grabbed his wrist and permitted him to hoist her onto the saddle, her long arms wrapping tight around his waist. "Get us out of here! Where there's one there are usually more!"

As if to prove her right, out of a thicket to the north of the first bowman flew two more arrows, whizzing toward the Ovaro.

"Hang on!" Fargo exclaimed, hauling on the reins. Both shafts missed. Applying his spurs, he felt her full bosom mold against his shoulder blades and caught a tantalizing whiff of her musky perfume. He raced after her Palomino, which had just disappeared into the forest to the south.

The woman's breath fluttered warmly on the nape of Fargo's neck and he found himself thinking of her enticing full red lips when he should have been concentrating on the task of staying alive.

No more arrows were fired. The stallion gained the sanctuary of the woods without further mishap but Fargo didn't slow until they had traveled a couple of hundred yards. He lost sight of the frantic Palomino, which was still fleeing at a breakneck pace.

Reining up, Fargo wheeled the pinto to check their back trail. "I don't think they're after us."

"First Julius, now Caesar!" the woman declared, staring in the direction her mount had gone.

"Ma'am?" Fargo absently asked while extracting cartridges from his gunbelt to replace those he had used.

"The Palominos my father gave me for my birthday four years ago. Julius was stolen by the savages a month ago, and now poor Caesar might be badly hurt!"

"You named your horses after an old Roman?" Even

Fargo had heard of the renowned leader of old, but he chuckled just the same.

"What's wrong with that?" the blonde said a trifle indignantly. "I love to study history, Roman history in particular. Julius Caesar was one of the greatest leaders who ever lived. I'd wager he was every bit as big and broad-shouldered as you."

"If you say so," Fargo said to be polite. Done reloading, he twirled the Colt into its holster and trotted on after her horse.

"I'm Lucy Brunsdale, by the way. I gather that you are one of my father's men?"

Fargo looked over his shoulder. Up close she was even more stunning, her eyes as blue as the deepest spring, her teeth snowy white. He imagined running his tongue over them, then chided himself for behaving like an awestruck sixteen-year-old. "No, I'm not."

A wariness crept over Lucy's features and she eased several inches back. "You're not? I'd assumed you were. My father doesn't like strangers roaming our land."

"So I've heard."

"Who are you? What are you doing here?"

Fargo introduced himself, thinking her father would have mentioned him, but Lucy plainly had never heard his name.

"Don't misunderstand, mister. I'm grateful for what you did. You saved my life, and my father will reward you handsomely."

"Any idea who I saved you from?" Fargo inquired. It had to be Indians, but to the best of his recollection, none of the tribes in Oregon were on the war path.

"We call them the Phantoms."

Fargo looked over his shoulder again and arched an eyebrow.

"I'm serious. No one knows who they are or why they're killing people. About five months ago it started. The Carter brothers were doing a timber survey for my father and didn't return when they should. So a search party was sent out. Both men had been horribly butchered in their tents." Lucy placed her hands on his shoulders. "Since then fourteen people have died. The only clues have been moccasins prints and a few arrows left in the bodies."

"Someone must know which tribe it is," Fargo insisted.

"Shows how bright you are. No white man has ever set foot in this region before. The trappers shunned it because there aren't enough beaver to speak of. Ranchers want nothing to do with it because there's not enough good graze for their cattle. And the farmers can't be bothered to clear trees for farming when there's plenty of prime farm elsewhere for the taking."

"Did anyone question friendly local tribes?"

"As a matter of fact, yes. The Calapooyans are the closest. They live down in the Willamette Valley. They say this area is bad medicine, that their people never come up here. My father talked to their chief and the chief is as stumped as we are."

"What does the army say?"

"They're next to worthless. Fort Hoskins is the only post within hundreds of miles. My father sent a rider to ask for help and the army sent a patrol under Captain Barker. He's been scouring the mountains for weeks now and hasn't turned up a thing."

The whole affair sounded peculiar to Fargo but he decided to reserve judgment until he learned more. A whinny up ahead alerted him they had caught up to the Palomino, and he spotted the animal in heavy brush, its dangling reins tangled fast.

"Caesar!" Lucy exclaimed, pushing off the Ovaro. She ran to the horse and lavished kisses on its neck. "Oh, Caesar! I was so worried. I couldn't bear to lose you after losing Julius."

Fargo couldn't help thinking how enjoyable it would be if he were the object of her affection. Climbing down, he examined the arrow imbedded in the pommel. It hadn't gone all the way through. Grasping the ash shaft, he wrenched upward and out came a barbed point similar to those used by tribes along the coast. The feathers were from an eagle. He hoped to find markings that would identify the tribe or owner but the shaft was bare.

"I hope you won't hold this against me," Lucy Brunsdale said.

"Hold what?" Fargo said, rotating, and stared into the muzzle of a derringer. "Is this how you show gratitude?"

"I don't think you're out to harm me. I honestly don't. But a gal can't take needless chances, can she? Undo your gunbelt and hand it over. I promise you'll get it back soon."

Fargo was tired of people pointing guns at him. He slowly lowered his left hand to his buckle, and then, while she was watching him pretend to loosen it, he lashed out with the arrow, smacking it hard against her wrist, so hard she yelped in pain and involuntarily pressed her forearm to her stomach. Seizing her wrist, he twisted it none-too-gently. Again she yelped, and dropped the derringer.

"Damn you! My father will gut you for this!" Lucy's other hand speared at his eyes, her fingers hooked to claw and rend.

Sidestepping, Fargo shifted his hold on the arrow so the barbed point was inches from her bosom. "Don't tempt me."

Lucy's cheeks flushed a vivid scarlet and she balled her fists. "If I were a man, I'd box your ears in!"

"A lot have tried," Fargo mentioned, pointing at the Palomino. "Now climb on. You're taking me to your father."

"Like hell I am," Lucy replied. "It'll be a cold day in hell before I do anything for you." She folded her arms across her chest.

"Maybe you'd rather I stab your horse?" Fargo bluffed.

"You would hurt Caesar?" Lucy blurted in horror as she threw her arm up over the animal's neck. "I misjudged you. I gave you the benefit of the doubt, but you're no better than the Phantoms."

"If you say so." Fargo picked up the derringer, stuffed it into a pocket, and forked the Ovaro. "Daylight is wasting. Don't keep me waiting."

Grumbling under her breath in a most unladylike manner, Lucy stepped into the stirrups and headed to the northwest.

"Hold it," Fargo said. It was his understanding the Brunsdale place was due west, at the base of the foothills flanking the Cascades. "Your home is that way." He nodded.

"My father isn't there," Lucy said, continuing on. "He's at the line camp overseeing the hunt for the Phantoms." She paused. "How it is you know so much about my family all of sudden? You've never been to our place before that I know of."

"Everyone knows about your father and his famous Timber Syndicate," Fargo said. Which wasn't entirely true. He had never heard of Luther Brunsdale until the letter arrived, but then, he seldom read a newspaper and had little interest in big business and high finance.

"They think they do," Lucy said with unaccountable bitterness.

"You don't sound all that happy about the empire he's created," Fargo casually observed, quoting Tom Poteet. Anything to keep her talking and take her mind off how mad she was at him.

"I was five when my father brought us out here," Lucy revealed. "My mother didn't want to leave Ohio but he insisted, so like a good little wife she obeyed. We weren't here a year when she died."

"Life on the frontier is rough," Fargo conceded. Especially for women, who toiled at backbreaking chores from dawn until dusk, day in and day out, year after year, until their bodies were stooped from wear and tear and their hair turned gray before their time.

"It wasn't that. My mother died of a broken heart. She hated Oregon and wanted to go back to Ohio but my father refused. By then the syndicate had been formed, and he couldn't very well leave his investors in the lurch, now could he?"

The crack of a twig reminded Fargo of the attack in the meadow. Lucy heard it, too, and reined up and looked at him. "We'll swing to the west to be safe," he whispered. "No more talking."

Lucy didn't argue. For a quarter of an hour they threaded through alders, oaks, and more madrones. Once they flushed a long-eared rabbit that sped off in gigantic leaps, spooking the skittish Palomino. It neighed and acted up, snorting and dancing until Lucy brought it under control.

As they moved on, Fargo noticed the woods were unnaturally quiet. The birds, the squirrels, even the insects were still, as if all of Nature were holding its collective breath. The tension was contagious. Fargo sucked the Henry from its saddle scabbard and rested the stock on his leg.

Suddenly Lucy drew rein and extended her arm toward a dense cluster of Sitka spruce. "I saw something move!" she whispered.

"What was it?" Fargo asked, bringing the Ovaro to a stop next to the Palomino.

"I can't rightly say. But I think it was on two legs."

"You think?" Fargo tucked the Henry to his shoulder and kneed the stallion forward a few yards. He estimated they were well over a mile from the meadow. It was doubtful the warriors had overtaken them, let alone gotten around in front of them without him being aware of it.

"See anything?" Lucy nervously asked.

Fargo shook his head. He was about to chalk it up to her imagination when he glimpsed a pair of dark, fierce eyes fixed on him from deep within the undergrowth. One instant they were there, the next they were gone, but there was no mistaking them for anything other than what they were.

Reining the pinto around, Fargo bellowed, "Back! Back the way we came!"

As Lucy hauled on the Palomino, an arrow buzzed out of nowhere and sank into the bole of a spruce almost at her elbow.

Swiveling, Fargo fired at where he had seen the eyes. Another shaft clipped the whangs on his right sleeve. A third came close to transfixing the Ovaro's neck. With a slap of his legs, he shot out of there, puzzled that the warriors never whooped, never showed themselves. It was almost as if he were fighting Apaches, but that couldn't be. He was over a thousand miles from their haunts in Arizona and New Mexico.

The Palomino pounded up a short slope and Lucy cut to the left. Fargo would rather have gone to the right but he let her do as she wanted in the belief she knew the countryside better.

The next second a rifle cracked, and Lucy Brunsdale cried out and pitched from the saddle.